"I'm Too Old for Careless Encounters,"

Cannon breathed into her mouth, "and so are you. If you let me have you, it's going to mean a commitment. Do you hear me? It won't be just sex."

"I love you," she whispered back. "I love you . . ."

"I'll never let you go, Margie," he vowed as he carried her down the long, dark hall. "Not as long as I live."

"Don't hurt me," she whispered, a last tiny surge of fear trembling through her.

"Sweet treasure," he murmured huskily, "that's the one thing I'm not going to do. . . ."

DIANA PALMER

is a prolific romance writer who got her start as a newspaper reporter. Accustomed to the daily deadlines of a journalist, she has no problem with writer's block. In fact, she averages a book every two months. Mother of a young son, Diana met and married her husband within one week: "It was just like something from one of my books."

Dear Reader:

SILHOUETTE DESIRE is an exciting new line of contemporary romances from Silhouette Books. During the past year, many Silhouette readers have written in telling us what other types of stories they'd like to read from Silhouette, and we've kept these comments and suggestions in mind in developing SILHOUETTE DESIRE.

DESIREs feature all of the elements you like to see in a romance, plus a more sensual, provocative story. So if you want to experience all the excitement, passion and joy of falling in love, then SILHOUETTE DESIRE is for you.

I hope you enjoy this book and all the wonderful stories to come from SILHOUETTE DESIRE. I'd appreciate any thoughts you'd like to share with us on new SILHOUETTE DESIRE, and I invite you to write to us at the address below:

Karen Solem
Editor-in-Chief
Silhouette Books
P.O. Box 769
New York, N.Y. 10019

DIANA PALMER
Fire And Ice

Silhouette Desire
Published by Silhouette Books New York
America's Publisher of Contemporary Romance

Other Silhouette Books by Diana Palmer

Heather's Song
The Cowboy and the Lady
September Morning
Friends and Lovers

SILHOUETTE BOOKS, a Division of Simon & Schuster, Inc.
1230 Avenue of the Americas, New York, N.Y. 10020

Copyright © 1983 by Diana Palmer

Distributed by Pocket Books

ISBN: 0-671-46823-5

First Silhouette Books printing August, 1983

10 9 8 7 6 5 4 3 2 1

America's Publisher of Contemporary Romance

Printed in the U.S.A.

To Nancy and Rodney,
  Luke, Jason, Tammy and Edith

Fire
And Ice

1

·ᴠᴏᴏᴏᴏᴏᴏᴏᴏᴏᴏᴏᴏᴏ·

Margie Silver had known she would draw interested glances from male diners in the exclusive Atlanta restaurant where she sat waiting. The vivid color of the green satin dress she wore was stunning enough in itself, but the cut was its real attraction. Long-sleeved, the wraparound dress had a plunging neckline, and its front edges were joined only by a wide belt at the waist. The effect, with Margie's long black hair and green eyes, was dynamite. The skirt peeked open to above the knee, revealing long, graceful legs, clad in sheer nylon stockings, that tapered down to small feet in sexy black high heels.

She sipped a glass of ginger ale, held in long, artistic fingers with pink-tipped nails. Margie might have looked like a high-fashion model, but she made her living writing sensuous historical romance novels as the notorious Silver McPherson. She wasn't allowed to mention that fact tonight, however, because revelation of her flamboyant alter ego might put a damper on her sister Jan's new romance. She had a hunch that this spur-of-the-moment dinner invitation cloaked a confrontation with Jan's future brother-in-law, the tycoon, and Margie had deliberately set out to provoke, choosing her dress to startle.

Margie's full red lips pursed irritatedly. She'd been in the middle of writing a particularly difficult scene when Jan called, breathlessly demanding to be met at the restaurant at seven. It was now half past seven, Jan was nowhere in sight, and Margie was furious.

She shifted in her chair, looking down at the satin dress in amusement. Jan would be horrified. She'd tried to impress on Margie the Van Dynes' very conservative public image, and the older brother's opinion of brassy women. She'd cautioned her older sister to be demure and had suggested that she dress like a nun. So naturally, Margie, being Margie and hating anything that sounded like an order, dragged out her brassiest dress and proceeded to use makeup like a sixty-year-old tart on the town.

Imagining Jan's reaction—to say nothing of young Andrew Van Dyne's and his elder brother's —made her eyes sparkle. If Jan had really sprung an impromptu meeting between them, Margie was going to enjoy herself.

"Oh, Margie, please act your age!" Jan would groan when Margie did something characteristically zany—like standing that nude statue of Venus in the middle of the flower garden where poor old Mrs. James would be shocked by it every afternoon on her way to water her own flowers. At least the photo inside the cover of her latest novel, *Blazing Passion*, was only of her face—Margie had threatened to have it done in a negligee, and Jan had threatened to leave the country.

But Margie would go right ahead living as she pleased and thinking up new ways to shock Jan. Margie's brief marriage had been responsible for much of that wild behavior. Her zaniness was a kind of camouflage to keep the world at bay, to cover her vulnerability. The sudden death of her husband after two long months of marriage had been almost a relief, leaving her disillusioned about men and intimacy and marriage. It had taught her one very real lesson— that you never knew other people until you lived with them. And she had every reason in the world to remember it.

She'd thought herself in love with Larry Silver. He was young and seemed to have a pleasant personality and a promising future as an attorney. They dated briefly, got married and soon discovered that they were completely unsuited to one another. When he died in a plane crash two months later, she had felt more guilt-ridden over the failed marriage than heartbroken. That had happened five years ago, when Margie was just twenty; she hadn't taken life seriously since. It was, she told

Jan, mental suicide to be serious, although she often thought that her younger sister saw right through her.

She took another sip of the ginger ale and sighed. If Jan and Andy didn't arrive in the next ten minutes, she was leaving. She had a month left to meet her publisher's deadline, and she didn't have time for socializing with strangers. Despite Jan's growing attachment to Andy, Margie had no desire to meet his brother.

She glared around her, feeling trapped. She knew "the tycoon," as she had dubbed him, disapproved of his brother's involvement with Jan. Jan was working as a legal secretary. The tycoon, however, wanted his brother matched with the debutante daughter of some Chicago society friends—not a nameless little Atlanta secretary. The debutante's people were in retail clothing, while the Van Dynes were clothing manufacturers. It would be a merger made in heaven for Andrew's brother.

She felt a tingling at the back of her neck, and turned to find herself staring into the piercing dark eyes of a man in the doorway. The impact of those scowling eyes, even across the width of the room, almost made her drop her glass. She'd never seen eyes like that, in a face like that. The man was huge, and he had a broad, hard face that might have been carved out of teak. His eyes were instantly hostile. Margie found herself fascinated by them. Why should a total stranger stare at her like that, with such open antagonism?

The disapproval on his face amused her and without thinking, she pursed her full lips and formed a very visible kiss, batting her long eyelashes and then sending him a come-hither smile before she turned back around.

She put down her glass to smother an attack of laughter. The look on that man's face had been worth gold. Bored and irritated herself, she was just beginning to enjoy this. Jan was going to be horrified when she learned how her sister had been passing the time.

A shadow fell across her, and she looked up to find the stranger looming over her with a face so stern it would have stopped traffic.

"Well, if it isn't Mount Rushmore," Margie murmured with a wicked smile. She half turned, leaning one arm over the back of her chair to look him up and down. "Sit down, honey, and have a drink with me."

He didn't smile. He looked as if he never had. His eyes wandered over her with growing disapproval. "No thanks. I have a prior engagement with a young lady." He stressed the last word, as if to imply that it could not be applied to Margie.

She liked his voice immediately. It was deep and faintly rough, very masculine and cultured. "Blind date?" She laughed.

He shook his head. "Social obligation," he said as though it were a distasteful one.

"Well, I'm a native," she drawled. "I might know her."

He looked as if he seriously doubted that. "Her name is Janet Banon."

Margie blinked. "Jan's my sister," she said without thinking, sitting up straight. Her eyes sized him up again, registering the returning hostility in his face. "What do you want with my sister?"

Instead of answering, he pulled out a chair and sat down as if he owned the table. He signaled a nearby waiter. "Bring me a scotch on the rocks," he told the white-jacketed waiter. "And a . . . Tom Collins for the lady," he added, glancing at the tall glass in her hand.

"Yes, sir," the waiter said politely, departing.

"And I take back the last word of that sentence," the man told Margie evenly. "A lady doesn't make blatant advances to strange men in restaurants."

Margie's green eyes sparkled. "You wrong me, sir," she said in her best Georgia drawl. "When I make advances to a man, I always take my clothes off first."

He cocked an eyebrow, appraising the expanse of skin visible in the long slit of her neckline. "I can't imagine that that would give you any advantage," he said flatly.

Always conscious of her small measurements, she glared at him. "Are you always so forthright?" she asked.

"Play with fire and you get burned," he replied curtly. His dark eyes pinned hers. "I don't like permissive women who dress like tarts. Nor do I care for women who get drunk before a meal and solicit men."

"How dare you . . . !" she began tritely, lost for words.

"Shut up," he said with the kind of authority that commanded instant obedience, even from renegade romance authors.

He paused until the waiter, depositing their drinks along with a check, had departed before he lifted his dark head to glare at her. "I understand that my brother wants to marry your sister. Over my dead body."

She gave him a quick glance. "Andrew's older brother?" she asked politely. "The one who makes women's underthings?" she added with a wicked smile.

If she had hoped to embarrass him, she didn't succeed. He leaned back in his chair, sipping his scotch, watching her with unblinking dark eyes. "We make a superior line of undergarments," he replied. His gaze fell once again on the bodice of her dress. "Along with a lightly padded bra that would do wonders for you."

The ginger ale sloshed out of the glass all over her napkin and part of the tablecloth, while her face flushed for the first time in five years.

"You'll have to excuse God for my shortcomings; he threw me together between wars," she growled.

He flexed his broad shoulders, and she noticed for the first time the elegant cut of his evening clothes, and how well black and white suited him. He was a fashion plate—not quite handsome, not really young—but hardly over the hill, either. Margie judged him to be about forty, or slightly under. Those hard lines in his face were the marks of high pressure, not age. He had the look of a human bulldozer.

"Why isn't your sister here?" he asked coldly.

Margie also leaned back, staring at him. "Jan didn't give me any explanations. She asked me to meet her here at seven and hung up. You know as much about it as I do. Probably more," she added wickedly. "I understand you tell your brother what clothes to put on every morning when he gets up. Do you also tell him which girls to date?"

His head tilted slightly to one side and his eyes narrowed. "Shall I be blunt?" he asked quietly. "Your sister would fit into my family the way a dormouse would fit into a cat convention. My world—and Andrew's—is best described as a social round of civilized warfare. Your sister, from what I've seen, couldn't fight her way out of a domestic dispute."

"Oh, I don't know," Margie replied thoughtfully. "She used to play tackle football when we were kids, and she still tells *me* what to do."

"You look as if you could use some guidance," he replied with maddening carelessness, staring pointedly at the dress.

"It's a designer dress," she returned.

"It would probably look better on the designer."

"He's a man."

"Exactly."

She took a deep breath and her eyes glittered. "Well, Mr. Undergarment Tycoon, you'll just have to excuse me. It's pretty obvious Jan got me here to meet you, and now that I've had that dubious honor, I'm going home."

She started to stand up, but a steely hand caught her wrist and jerked her back down. She was startled as much by the unexpected action as by the tingle of pleasure that ran up her arm at his touch.

"Not yet," he said in a deep, low tone. "My brother isn't marrying your sister. I'll see to it."

"I couldn't be more pleased," she replied hotly. "Because I don't want bad blood in my family, either!"

"Watch it, honey. I bite," he cautioned.

"On the neck?" she asked with a venomous smile.

"Andy and I are going down to Florida to visit our mother for a few weeks," he mused. "That should cool his ardor. And I don't think there's much danger of your sister following him."

"Why?" Margie demanded. "Because she's a secretary with a low bank balance?"

"Something like that."

"For your information," she said softly, "I can afford to charter her a plane to Florida if that's what she wants. And I will. Not that I want Andy for a brother-in-law, you understand," she added. "But because I don't like stuffed shirts with big bank accounts telling my family what to do."

His eyes were calculating. "Drawing battle lines?" he asked softly. "I've never lost a skirmish, Miss Banon."

"My name isn't Banon," she said stiffly. "It's Silver."

He cocked an eyebrow, glancing at her ringless left hand. "My condolences to your husband, although I'd bet good money that you're no longer living with him." He laughed shortly when she blushed. "On the button, I presume?" He sat forward, leaning his forearms on the table, and his eyes were threatening. "I don't intend for Andy to marry your sister, regardless of whether or not there's money in your family. It wouldn't work. I don't want another broken marriage to add to my mother's heartaches."

Her own eyes went to his ringless left hand and she smiled demurely. "No longer living with your wife?" she asked.

His face went harder, if that was possible. "I rue the day I agreed to let Andrew manage the Atlanta branch of the company," he said coldly, getting gracefully to his feet. "But fortunately, it's a problem I can solve. Keep out of it, Mrs. Silver. I won't tolerate your interference."

"What will you do, Mr. Van Dyne, honey, have me flogged?" she asked with a sweet smile. "Why don't you pack your little ole carpetbag and go back up Nawth where you belong?"

He lifted an eyebrow. "If you're going to toss old history at me, Silver, you'd better remember who won that war. *Ciao.*" And he walked away, leaving her with the bill.

"Leaving me to pay the bill," she grumbled when Jan returned to the Victorian house she shared with Margie. "Calling me names, threatening to break up you and Andy . . . what kind of man is he?"

"A law unto himself." Jan sighed, dropping down on the couch. "Oh, Margie, I had such high hopes that if I didn't show up with Andy, you and Cannon might hit it off. . . ."

"Cannon?" she asked, arching her eyebrows.

"That's his name, although most people call him 'Cal,' " Jan said miserably. "I'm sorry, really I am. You see, Andy wants to invite me down to the family's beach house in Panama City, Florida for a couple of weeks. I want to go, so that I can get to know Andy's mother, but Cannon won't hear of it. He's been so dead set against our getting married, and I thought"—she glanced at Margie and grimaced—"well, I thought meeting you might change his mind. You can charm anyone when you set your mind to it. I didn't realize you were going dressed like a hooker," she added regretfully.

Margie struck a pose. "I must be getting better as an actress." She grinned. "I sure convinced your future brother-in-law that my reputation was in shreds."

"Margie!" came the groaned reply.

"Are you sure you want to marry Andy?" Margie asked with genuine concern. "Just think, you'd have to go through life having that human bulldozer order you around."

"We wouldn't have to see Cannon all that often," Jan assured her. "He lives in Chicago, you know."

She turned away, toying with a statuette on the mantle. "Is he married?" she asked carelessly.

"Not anymore. His wife was making time with just about everything in pants. He divorced her, and Andy says the only use he has for women now isn't printable."

"I can't imagine any woman desperate enough to get in *his* bed," Margie retorted, her eyes glittering.

"They say he's much sought-after in Chicago," Jan mused, watching her sister's reaction with great interest.

"Well, he wouldn't be in Atlanta," Margie grumbled. "And never by me!"

Jan shook her head and frowned. Margie was a lot like Cannon Van Dyne, her sister thought, although she probably didn't realize it. Margie hid her inner feelings under all that clowning, but she wasn't as carefree as she pretended. Jan had been there the day Lawrence Silver died in that plane crash, and only she knew the truth about Margie's unhappy marriage. Margie had avoided men ever since, except on a friendly basis. She wanted no one near enough to hurt her again.

But she seemed to be reacting to Cannon in a totally alien way. Margie wasn't usually antagonistic, but her eyes glittered when she mentioned Andy's brother. It was the most violent emotion she'd shown in five years.

"Cannon's an attractive man," Jan murmured.

"That big stone wall?" Margie turned away. "I don't even want to talk about him. Imagine, leaving me the bill for his scotch and water, and ordering me a drink I didn't even touch! I ought to have the bill embedded in a block of concrete and mailed to him special delivery, collect." Her green eyes brightened. "I wonder how I could do it. . . ."

Jan couldn't repress a grin. Margie was incorrigible.

The jangling of the phone cut into the conversation. Jan ran for it, her eyes lighting up at once when she held the receiver to her ear.

"It's Andy," she whispered to Margie, who nodded and left the room, knowing her sister would appreciate some privacy.

She wandered out into the long hall. On the way to her bedroom, her eyes fell on the wood umbrella stand she and Larry had bought soon after their wedding. They'd been browsing in an antique store—Margie's passion for the past irritated him, and he'd only gone under protest—when her eyes had fallen on the handcarved wooden relic. She'd bought it against his wishes, because it had been expensive. She'd argued that she had money of her own, a little that her grandmother McPherson had left her, and he'd stormed out of the shop in a huff, leaving her to handle the transaction.

They'd had a violent argument about it that night, and he'd forced her in bed—not for the first time—leaving her hurt and bruised and frightened. The next morning he'd dressed to go on his fatal trip while she studied him with tormented eyes. She'd watched him leave the room with the most incredible kind of pain in her heart, wondering what had happened to their marriage, longing to be free of him.

She shuddered at the memory, glaring down at the umbrella stand. Why had she left it here, in a house that now held no memento of him, not even a picture? Perhaps it was some subconscious thing, she told herself, to keep alive the guilt that had never gone away. She'd wished herself free, and he'd died. Somehow, she felt responsible for the plane crash—despite the fact that she had had nothing to do with it.

She stared down at the antique. Perhaps she'd give it to Mrs. James next door. She smiled as she went into her blue and white bedroom. Mrs. James was really a doll, despite her strict puritanical streak and her fervent disapproval of her notorious neighbor. Margie actually encouraged that disapproval, for reasons she'd never worked out. She wasn't really the uninhibited creature her readers believed her to be. The woman inside the flamboyant shell was actually very vulnerable, and achingly lonely. But her marriage had taught her one thing—that appearances were not to be trusted. She never wanted to take the chance of being trapped again. She never wanted another domineering man in her life, and even as the thought registered, she saw a mental picture of Cannon Van Dyne. She shivered involuntarily. He was like Larry, she thought. All arrogant command, the kind of man who'd want a clinging, obedient woman with no independence and no spirit. He'd smother her. . . .

The bedroom door burst open as Margie was drawing her mint green nightgown over her head, and she turned, smiling at Jan's excited face. Her younger sister so rarely glowed like that. Jan was such a shy, gentle creature.

"Oh, Margie, we've got another chance!" she said, eyeing her older sister warily.

"We?" Margie asked with raised eyebrows. She smoothed the gown over her hips and rested her hands on them. "Okay, shrimp, what have you got me into this time?"

Jan sat down on the bed, running a nervous

everyone to be as happy as she was. But she didn't know how to help her sister.

"We've gotten off the track," Margie murmured, the smile back on her face like magic. "What were you so excited about? A chance to make Mount Rushmore change his mind?"

Jan blinked. "Mount Rushmore?"

"Cannon Van Dyne."

"Uh, yes, actually." Her eyes were wary after the long conversation, and she hesitated. "Andy's made a dinner reservation for four at Louis Dane's tomorrow night."

Margie straightened and walked over to the curtains, her back as stiff as old Mrs. McPherson's. "Four?"

Jan nodded. "You, me, Andy . . ."

"And . . . ?"

Jan swallowed. "Cannon Van Dyne."

2

Margie's green eyes took on a peculiar glitter as she said, "No! Absolutely not!"

"You both got off to a bad start," Jan reminded her. "And you helped—you know you did—with that horrible dress. I wasn't deserting you; I just thought if the two of you were left alone together . . ." She groaned. "Oh, I made a mess of it myself by not telling you why I wanted you to go to the restaurant. But Margie, you don't know how important Cannon's approval is. I can't ask Andy to give up his family and his inheritance all at once just for my sake. I can't!" She gave Margie a pleading glance. "And I can't fight Cannon alone; I'm not strong enough. I can't even pretend that I've got a chance against him."

"And you think I have?" Margie asked.

"Yes, because you aren't afraid of him," Jan said. "I've seen you charm men. When you turn on that smile and act like yourself, you draw them like flies."

Margie looked shocked. "If you think I'd deliberately lead that bulldozer on . . ."

"I wouldn't ask you to," Jan said quickly. "Never would I do that to you. But you have a knack for getting people to listen to you, for drawing them out. You could convince Cannon that I'm not too young and stupid and unaccomplished to become a Van Dyne," she continued, unabashed.

"I'm not sure I want you to become one," Margie said with a flash of resentment. "You know very well how I feel about cliques and snobbery. And for that matter, don't you think it's time you told Andy about Dad's drinking? You can't hide your past forever."

Jan nodded her head, looking guilty for a moment. "I know. I was hoping to tell him down in Panama City. It's just that our backgrounds are so different. And Cannon doesn't think I can cope with their lifestyle—or make Andy happy."

"You most certainly could," Margie argued. "You have poise and terrific manners. And you learned how to organize dinner parties for your boss, with his wife's help. . . ."

"See?" Jan grinned. "You're already sure I could make the grade. All you have to do is sell me to Cannon."

"Slavery was abolished by Lincoln," Margie pointed out.

"Margie!"

"The tycoon wouldn't listen," came the sullen reply. "He's a card-carrying chauvinist with delusions of upper-crust grandeur. So arrogant . . . imagine, a man who makes ladies' underthings being arrogant!" Her face contorted and she burst into giggles. "Jan, suppose you get Andy to filch me a lacy set of underwear for my statue of Venus . . . imagine what Mrs. James would say!"

Jan couldn't repress a laugh. Margie, in this mood, was hilarious. "Okay, I'll do it. Now will you please come to dinner with us tomorrow night? Maybe you can get me that invitation to Panama City."

Margie sighed. "Has it ever occurred to you that I might be more of a detriment to you than an asset? I ought to be horsewhipped for deliberately giving him the wrong impression tonight. I don't even know why I did it." She groaned, swinging back her long, tangled hair. "It's this awful deadline I'm on, with only a month to go, and the book isn't going well at all. . . ." Her eyes met Jan's. "Darling, I'm sorry. I'll try to make amends tomorrow night. I'll bite my tongue in half if it will help, truly I will. And one way or another, we'll get you that invitation to Panama City!"

"I knew you wouldn't let me down," Jan said affectionately. She hugged her sister hard. "It will all work out. You'll see."

But as Margie dressed for dinner the following evening, she wasn't convinced of that. She stared at her reflection in the mirror with grave misgivings.

Her dress was simple—a mass of black chiffon

with a slightly sensuous v-neck surrounded by ruffles. She had put her rebellious black hair in a high knot on top of her head, with wisps falling around her face, and schooled herself to look sedate. She was sparing with her makeup and chose a perfume with a light, flowery, almost innocent scent. She looked so different from the practiced seductress of the previous night that she imagined Cannon Van Dyne might not even recognize her.

When Jan saw her irrepressible sister, she had to smother a laugh. "My, what a difference," she said. "You remind me of Grandmother McPherson."

"Well, it's her house. Or it was." She sighed. "I guess some of her rubbed off on me. At least this won't shock your horrible future brother-in-law."

"Care to bet?" Jan grinned.

Margie sighed, noticing how lovely Jan looked in her pale green sheath dress with its matching accessories. She was so radiant, so obviously in love with her Andy. Margie liked Andy herself. He was so open and friendly.

"Well, shall we go down?"

"Better, I guess," Jan said. "They'll be here any minute."

Margie went downstairs into the living room with her sister and sat nervously on the edge of the sofa.

"Will you relax?" Jan teased. "I'm the one who should be nervous. I've never been around Cannon for longer than the time it took to say hello."

The doorbell rang suddenly, and Margie actually jumped.

Jan stared at her incredulously. She'd never seen

Margie so keyed up. "It's okay," she soothed, touching her sister's rigid shoulder as she went to answer the door.

Margie stood up, gathering her nerve. He wouldn't get the best of her, she thought stubbornly. She wouldn't let him put her down again.

She heard voices: Andy's pleasant, friendly one —and a deeper, harsher one.

Her fingers clutched her purse as Andy came into the room, followed by Cannon. Andy was almost Cannon's height, but he lacked the bulk and muscular trim of his older brother. He had light brown hair and light brown eyes, and a face that combined strength and tenderness. He was good-looking, but Jan obviously thought he was the handsomest man alive—if her expression was anything to go by. Andy put a protective arm around her and bent to kiss her softly, despite Cannon's disapproving glare.

"I think I've got that invitation—from Mother herself," Andy whispered to Jan before he lifted his head. "Evening, Margie," he added in a louder voice.

"Good evening," Margie said quietly, her nervous gaze going to Cannon. He was taking in her appearance with an I-don't-believe-it stare, and seemed to have missed the hushed exchange between Andy and Jan.

Cannon looked more formidable than ever. His evening clothes accentuated his masculinity until it was threatening. The dark material clung to powerful muscles that seemed to ripple under the expensive cloth as he moved. He was graceful for a man his size, and light on his feet. His hands were dark and big, and beautiful in their own way. He wore only a single gold signet ring, and a thin, fabulously expensive gold watch nestled in the thick hairs at the back of his wrist. Margie wondered if the rest of his sensuous body was covered in that same dark hair, and she caught her breath at her uncharacteristic thought.

Cannon's thick hair gleamed almost black under the light; his deep-set brown eyes glared at Margie.

"Shall we go?" he asked brusquely. "I'd like to get an early night."

"God forbid that we should hold you up, Mr. Van Dyne," Margie said sweetly as she picked up her shawl and threw it around her shoulders.

"Don't worry, you won't," he said quietly, watching her. "I didn't picture you in a Victorian house, Mrs. Silver."

She lifted an eyebrow. "I can imagine what kind of house you did picture me in," she said with a faint smile. "Sorry to have shocked you."

"It will take more than your surroundings to convince me that my first impression wasn't more accurate," he replied.

"Why, Mr. Van Dyne, honey," Margie murmured, batting her long eyelashes, "how you do go on."

"You go on," he replied, standing aside to let her lead them through the door, "before I lose what little patience I have left."

Jan threw a worried glance her way, but Margie

didn't see it. She was already rushing to get out the door Cannon held open. She had a vague notion that he'd enjoy slamming it in her face.

The restaurant was crowded, but Cannon immediately attracted the attention of the maitre d', who seated them at a table beside an imitation waterfall, complete with lush vegetation.

"My God, the swamp," Andy muttered as Cannon ordered from the wine steward.

Margie grinned. "Did you think to bring mosquito netting?" she whispered.

"We may need one of those sticky strips to catch the bugs. . . ."

"Would you two children mind behaving while we're in public?" Cannon asked curtly, glaring from one to the other.

"Yes, Daddy," Margie said demurely, lowering her eyes.

Cannon seemed to swell with indignation as the waiter handed him a glass of wine from the bottle he'd ordered. He took a sip and nodded, waiting until the waiter filled the other glasses and left their menus before he spoke.

"You two may not be wildlife enthusiasts," Cannon commented gruffly, while Margie almost burst out laughing at the misapprehension, "but you might at least appreciate the engineering that was responsible for this waterfall."

Margie didn't dare look at Andy; it would have been disastrous. Instead, she buried her nose in the menu. "It's very nice," she agreed, with a straight face. "If they forget to bring water and glasses, we can always dip in here."

"Oh, Margie." Jan groaned, burying her face in her hands.

A smothered, strangled sound emerged from Andy's mouth before he slapped his napkin against it and faked a cough.

Cannon's big hands were crushing a part of the menu. "If either of you order anything with alcohol in it, I'll walk out and leave you," he told Andy and Margie. "My God, are you already high on the scent of the wine?"

Margie lifted her composed face and glared at him.

"Margie," Jan squeaked, "you did promise. . . ."

Margie nodded, moving the wine glass toward Cannon. "You're absolutely right, darling, I did. I won't even wade in the fountain this time," she added.

Cannon scowled at her. "How old did you say you were? Twelve?"

She lifted her eyebrows. "No fair," she said. "This is supposed to be an opportunity for us to learn to get along."

"It will take more than this," he said flatly.

"Amen," she agreed. "But I happen to be hungry, if you don't mind not spoiling my appetite. I skipped breakfast and lunch."

"That typewriter is going to be the death of you," Jan murmured, and caught herself barely in time. She'd begged Margie not to mention her profession just yet. Cannon had enough against the flamboyant brunette without putting such a weapon in his hands.

"Typewriter?" Cannon caught the word immediately and stared pointedly at Margie.

Margie thought fast. "I do a political opinion column for our local weekly newspaper," she said.

"And you skipped meals because that took all day?" he asked suspiciously.

"I do a political opinion column every week," she returned, "and I have to keep at least two weeks ahead in case I decide to run away to Bermuda with my latest boyfriend."

"God help your poor husband," he growled.

"My husband is dead, Mr. Van Dyne," she said quietly, sobering at once. "He was killed in an airplane crash five years ago. Now if you don't mind, it's a subject I'd rather we closed. It's very painful."

He looked embarrassed, studying her for a long moment before turning his disconcerting gaze to his menu.

Margie studied her own. Even though she could now afford the prices at better restaurants, these staggered her. Nothing was under twenty dollars and the least expensive item was a simple chicken breast stuffed with a ham and cheese filling. She wasn't fond of chicken, but she wasn't going to allow herself to be obligated to Cannon Van Dyne, even for a meal.

"Shall I translate for you?" Cannon asked with grudging politeness when the waiter returned and stood beside her.

She smiled with studied sweetness. "How kind," she murmured demurely, "but I think I can struggle through it." She looked up at the waiter. "*Je prends la poule cordon bleu, s'il vous plaît,*" she said in flawless French, "*des pommes de terre Louis et des choux de Bruxelles.*"

The waiter grinned at her, writing it all down. "*Avec plaisir, madame,*" he replied. "*Monsieur?*"

Cannon shot her a glare while he ordered himself a steak, a baked potato, and a green salad. The order was given in clipped English and he was still glaring at her when the waiter went around to take the rest of the order from Andy.

"Not bad," he said coolly, studying her. "Your French is quite good. Do you speak other languages?"

"Spanish," she told him. "Italian. A little Arabic and some Hebrew. I love languages. They were my passion when I went to college."

"What was your major?"

"Journalism," she said. "I only went for two years, though."

He frowned. "Why did you leave?"

Her face closed. "I got married."

"Margie's a gourmet cook," Jan told Cannon when the silence lingered after the waiter had departed. "She's quite good at it."

"Is she?" Cannon asked, glancing toward Margie. "What's your specialty?"

"Goose," she shot back.

Something flared briefly in his dark eyes. "Thinking of mine?" he murmured softly. "Forget it, honey, that's been tried by experts."

Her green eyes sparkled. "I do pretty well with buttered toadstools and deadly nightshade," she added. "But you'd probably thrive on that kind of diet."

"Margie!" Jan groaned.

"Don't worry about it," Cannon told the younger woman. "She can handle herself, and so can I." His dark eyes gleamed as he leaned back in his chair, carelessly holding the wineglass in his graceful hand. "I don't mind stimulating conversation at the dinner table. It's rather refreshing."

"Why?" Margie asked sweetly. "Do people usually dive under the table when they disagree with you?"

He cocked his head. "It's safer," he murmured.

"By the way," Andy interrupted, taking matters into his own hands, "I called Mother earlier this evening to tell her Jan was coming down to Panama City with us."

Cannon lifted a bushy eyebrow at Andy's confident tone. "So she told me. I had a conversation with her myself, and I've decided it might not be a bad idea for Jan to visit, after all. As a matter of fact, I suggested that Mrs. Silver might want to accompany her sister."

The three of them stared at him in surprise, Jan and Andy elated, Margie horrified. "I don't do a great deal of traveling, Mr. Van Dyne," she finally said quietly. "And I do have certain . . . obligations."

"You can take the typewriter with you," Jan promised, her eyes pleading. Margie knew her sister was hoping she wouldn't do anything to upset the apple cart.

Cannon's eyebrows rose. "Do you have some new kind of fetish?"

"I most certainly do not," Margie replied tightly. "I simply take my responsibilities seriously. The newspaper depends on my column. . . ."

"You may certainly bring your typewriter, then," he said.

"You can teach it to surf," Andy put in, grinning.

Margie grinned back. "I'm still trying to teach it the alphabet," she returned, winking at Jan.

"At least promise that you'll consider the invitation," Jan begged, and Margie nodded her agreement.

Cannon didn't say anything, but he watched her. It was unnerving, that steady, unblinking scrutiny. Against her will, she looked up, and found her gaze trapped. Some faint sensation began to flower inside her—a tickling along her nerves, a trembling excitement that she'd never before felt. Electricity seemed to flow from his eyes to hers, so that she had to tear her gaze away before she burned up.

She lifted her fork and almost dropped it. She was more unsettled than she'd thought, she told herself.

After dinner, they went across the street to a disco, where Margie found herself alone with Cannon when Jan and Andy wandered off to dance to the throbbing, deafening music.

Cannon lit a cigarette with steady fingers and sipped the coffee he'd ordered for himself and

Margie. He looked as out of place as Margie felt. She would rather have been back sitting by that little waterfall—she had only belittled it to irritate him.

"Having fun, honey?" he asked mockingly.

She gave him her sweetest smile. "Just as much fun as you are, Mr. Van Dyne," she replied, raising her voice to make him hear her. "Don't y'all just love this quaint little place?"

He glared at her and took another sip of his coffee. He apparently liked it black, because she hadn't seen him take cream all evening. It wasn't surprising. Somehow it suited his image.

"My God, I'm going deaf," he said after a minute, pushing the cup aside. He had an actor's voice, soft dark velvet even when it was raised. "Drink your coffee and let's get out of here."

She obeyed him only because the noise was deafening her, too. He went and said something to Andy before he came back to escort her out the door into the warm night air. She moved away from his hard fingers as soon as possible, disliking the sensations their touch caused on her bare arm.

"Where are we going?" she asked, glancing up at him. She was of above-average height, but it was a long way to his face. Just the sight of him would frighten away nine out of ten muggers, and she felt oddly safe with him.

He cocked an eyebrow and glanced down at her with a vague smile. "Forget it," he murmured, erroneously assuming that her look was flirtatious. "You're not well-rounded enough for my taste."

Her eyes felt as if they were bulging. "Mister, you

are not only insulting, you are insufferable," she bit out.

"What happened to the sweet little Southern belle I picked up at your home?" he queried.

"She's just fired off that cannon in Charleston harbor," she flared back. "And you can forget that hundred-year-old conflict. I don't lose."

His eyes gleamed back at her. "Neither do I."

"There's always a first time."

He chuckled softly as he escorted her back to the big Lincoln. He put her in the passenger side and climbed in at the wheel.

"Where are we going?" she asked again.

"Nowhere. I told Andy to finish that dance and come on out." He threw a careless arm across the back of the seat and looked, really looked, at her, until a faint flush rose in her cheeks.

"I have all my own teeth," she said. "And despite your opinion of it, everything you see is genuine."

"A far cry from the lady of the evening," he said, watching her eyes glitter at him. "Where did you put her?"

"Back into my Halloween bag of disguises," she muttered. She shrugged. "Jan told me to dress conservatively and rush down to that restaurant for dinner last night. I was in the middle of a . . . of something, and I didn't want to be dragged out. . . ."

"So you set out to embarrass her as much as possible?" he asked.

"I had a feeling she'd invited you and Andy," Margie admitted with a wry smile. "She'd told me you were very conservative yourself and that I must behave."

"Conservative." He mulled over the word and a faint smile momentarily softened the hard lines of his broad face. "I've been called a lot of things in my time, but I think conservative is a new one."

"You wear traditionally styled clothes and drive a classy car," she pointed out.

"It puts my adversaries into a false state of ease," he murmured.

She was beginning to realize that. He was a worrying puzzle; none of the prefabricated pieces she'd imagined him to be seemed to fit together.

"You're devious, Mr. Van Dyne," she said.

"I'm careful, Mrs. Silver," he returned. "If I make a mistake, people lose their jobs. I give the image the corporation needs—in public."

She studied the unyielding lines of his body. "And in private?" she asked absently.

He half turned in the seat and looked straight into her eyes. "Do you make a habit of flirting with strange men?" he asked, ignoring her question.

"Not really," she replied honestly. "You looked instantly hostile and disapproving. It got my dander up."

"You aren't used to disapproval?"

"Only from Mrs. James."

He blinked. "I beg your pardon?"

"My next-door neighbor," she explained with an impish smile. "Very strait-laced, like my grandmother McPherson, who raised Jan and me. She takes exception to my nude statue of Venus in the backyard."

His eyebrows shot up. "You keep a nude statue . . . I'm not surprised." He chuckled. "It does seem to fit the picture I'm getting of you."

And it was completely false, but she wasn't about to admit it. Let him think her flamboyant and forward and sensual. It would keep such a man at bay.

"Do you sell a lot of . . . underwear?"

He sat back up, looking intimidating and calculating and just faintly amused. "You'd better leave that subject, honey, or you may get in over your head. I'm a good fourteen years your senior, and I'd be willing to bet that I've done a hell of a lot more living than you have."

"I don't intimidate easily," she replied.

"I believe you. In fact, it makes you more interesting than I had thought at first. Women's lib may be all the rage these days, but I hate like hell to be chased and fawned over."

She studied his hard face for a long moment. "You are chased, aren't you?" she asked seriously. "Because you're wealthy and powerful, and some women would do anything to be part of that world."

He looked as if she'd surprised him—and he wasn't accustomed to surprises. "Yes," he replied.

"Is that what your wife married you for?" she asked quietly.

His eyes flared dangerously. "That's a subject I don't discuss."

"I'm sorry, I didn't mean to pry. I'm a rather private person myself," she admitted, finding him surprisingly easy to talk to.

He watched her, scowling, for a long time. He made her uneasy; he rattled her. She couldn't remember a man ever affecting her so violently.

"Enigma," he murmured absently. "You don't fit into the usual category."

"The line of women pleading to be taken into your bed?" she suggested. "Or did you have another category in mind?"

"If that was meant to shock, it fell short of the goal," he said softly. "You're very much on the defensive with me. Why?"

She didn't like the turn the conversation was taking. "Ladies don't discuss such subjects, anyway," she drawled.

"Oh, haul down the flag, Margie," he growled. "I'm tired of the pose. A little of that accent goes a long way."

Her eyes gleamed. "And I'm getting pretty tired of you, too, Mr. Tycoon. I don't like being taken apart and analyzed! And by the way, I find your accent just as grating as you seem to find mine, you carpetbagger!"

He burst out laughing. "Will it ease your mind if I tell that a grandmother of mine was born and raised in Charleston?"

"Not much, no," she said. She was losing this battle of words, and she didn't like it. He wasn't what she'd expected.

"What's wrong, honey, have you given up trying to charm me?"

She glanced at him. "I'd have more luck trying to charm a sweet potato," she commented.

He chuckled deep in his throat. "You might at that." He reached out suddenly and caught her shoulder, jerking her close enough to smell the rich fragrance of his cologne while his head tilted back and he looked down his arrogant nose at her. "Whether you know it or not, you're coming to Panama City. And if you try that sweet seduction on me again, you'd better remember something: I've been married and women are no strangers to my bed. I'm not a gentle lover, Margie."

She actually gasped at the insinuation. "As if I care," she managed weakly.

"I've known women like you," he said levelly, his eyes holding hers relentlessly. "You flirt and charm outrageously, but at the first sign of passion, you turn around and run. It took me a while to get your measure, but I've got it now, and you'd better look out. Throw yourself at me in Panama City and I'll take you on the damned beach."

She felt the threat all the way to her toes as he freed her and moved back into his own seat to light another cigarette, as calm as if he'd been out for a stroll. "And for the record, all your scheming isn't going to help your sister. There is no way, repeat no way," he said, his shadowed dark eyes like glittering slits, "that I am going to give my approval to that marriage."

"Then why invite us to Panama City? For target practice?"

"I have my reasons," he said enigmatically.

"You won't even give Jan a chance," she accused.

"I don't dare," he returned sharply. "I know the obstacles. You don't. Your way of life and mine are as different as New York and a swamp."

"You bloody Yankee!" she spat. She was beautiful in her fury, wild-eyed, flushed, her hair coming loose to stream down around her shoulders.

"Gloves off, Silver?" he taunted, drawing on the cigarette.

"As if I'd want my sister to marry into a family that produced a son like you," she cried. "I'd rather she died an old maid!"

He looked as if he were going to strangle trying not to laugh. Devil, straight out of hell, she thought furiously.

"Calm down, honey."

She wanted to attack him. She wanted to get her hands on him and beat him. It was the first time in her life she'd felt such physical rage.

He knew it, too. His eyes glittered with amusement.

"I want to go home," she ground out, dragging her eyes away from him to glare at the deserted parking lot. She felt tears wetting her long eyelashes, and hated him for being able to make her cry.

"Giving up?" he taunted.

She drew in a long, shuddering breath.

Incredibly, he laid the cigarette in the ashtray and pulled her into his arms. She was rigid and shocked, but he hauled her up against him and began rocking her slowly, gently. She let her taut muscles relax little by little until she could feel the soft swell of her breasts pressed against the warm wall of his chest.

"I won't go . . . to Panama City," she breathed, knowing Jan needed her support, but too afraid of him to risk it.

"Yes, you will," he said gently, his voice right at her ear so that she could feel his warm breath on her skin. "You'll go because I want you to go . . . and underneath, you want it, too," he whispered darkly.

She pushed against his chest and found herself panicking when she didn't regain her freedom.

"Oh, don't!" she pleaded quickly, pushing harder, her eyes widening. "Please, don't ever do that. . . ."

He let her go immediately, watching her struggle for composure.

"Is it me, or are you that way with all men?" he asked quietly.

"I can't bear to be trapped or held against my will," she admitted. "It terrifies me."

He glanced out the windshield to see Jan and Andy moving slowly toward them, hand in hand, and he cursed violently under his breath.

"Someday," he threatened softly, "you're going to tell me why."

"Don't bet on it," she advised, her composure returning with her temper. "If I come to Panama City, I expect to avoid you."

He smiled dangerously. "You're coming, all right," he told her. "If I have to carry you every step of the way."

"That's called kidnapping," she informed him. "It's illegal."

"I make my own rules. Didn't you know?" he

asked with magnificent arrogance. "What I want, I get."

"Not this time," she said.

"Especially this time," he returned. His eyes searched hers in the silence of the car and for a moment the world disappeared into their brown, shadowy depths.

She felt a sensation like fingers drifting across her bare skin as she stared back at him. Time seemed to freeze while she fought against an attraction she'd never known before. He was nothing like the picture her mind had formed of him. He was a renegade, an outlaw, a pirate who only lacked a patch over one eye. He was the biggest threat she'd ever faced, and part of her wanted to get out of the car and run. But another part, a nagging part, was intrigued by the budding of a slow, soft curiosity about him.

His finger reached out and touched, lightly, the softness of her bow-shaped mouth; a touch like a whisper, incredibly sensuous, as it eased just slightly between her lips and found the pearly whiteness of her teeth.

She drew back from him with a strange little gasp.

His wide, sensuous mouth curved mockingly. "Tell me you're coming to Panama City, Margie," he murmured as the younger couple approached the car. "Or I'll forbid Andy to bring your sister."

"You would!" she accused.

"Damned straight. Yes or no? Now!"

"Yes," she groaned. She looked away.

Andy opened the door and he and Jan climbed

into the back seat, both of them smiling and on top of the world.

"Where to now, big brother?" Andy laughed.

"Home," Cannon said, starting the car.

He let the Lincoln ease to a stop in front of Margie and Jan's house minutes later and cut the ignition. When they reached the door he turned to Margie, while Andy and Jan said a slow, sweet good night a few feet away.

"I'll pick you both up at six on Friday morning," he said quietly.

"If you'd just give me the flight number and the airline . . ." she faltered, hating her own fear of him.

"Flight number?" He smiled coolly. "I have my own jet, honey. I'm going to fly us down."

She knew that she was pale; she could feel the blood draining from her face. "I'd rather not. . . ."

"I've been flying for twenty years, Margie," he said with a tender note under the impatience. "I promise you I'm no daredevil when other lives depend on my actions." He studied her narrowly. "You haven't flown in a small aircraft since the crash that killed your husband?"

She studied his black tie. "No."

"I'll take care of you," he said in a strange, soft tone that brought her eyes up to his involuntarily.

She was caught in that deep brown web again and a dark sweetness filled her.

"Come with me," he murmured softly.

She tried to speak, but her breath caught. He was hypnotizing her, he was . . .

"I don't have a choice . . . do I?" she whispered unsteadily.

"No," he murmured absently. His eyes dropped to her soft, parted lips. "I haven't wanted a woman's mouth so much since my souped-up Chevy days," he said so that only she could hear him.

"That I wouldn't believe on a bet," she said, trying to make light of it when her pulse was jumping like a frightened rabbit.

"Wouldn't you?" He moved a step closer and her eyes dilated wildly. She'd already had a taste of his strength and it scared her. She didn't want to find out if that sensuous, faintly cruel mouth was as expert as it looked.

"You'd hurt . . ." she said without thinking. She couldn't think.

His eyes flashed down at hers and there was a matching wildness in them. "God, yes, I would," he muttered under his breath. "And you'd fight me like a wildcat, wouldn't you?"

She nodded slowly, unable to break the silver thread that bound them together. "Tooth and nail."

"For the first few minutes," he amended, letting his eyes drop slowly, boldly, over her body before they slid back up to meet her own. "After that . . ."

She cleared her throat. "I have an appointment Friday. . . ."

"Break it," he said curtly. "I meant what I said. If you back out, Jan doesn't come, either."

She searched his dark eyes, confused, uncertain. "Will you at least listen to me if I come?"

"Yes," he said, and she knew he meant it.

"Then I'll do it."

He lifted his chin slightly. "I won't promise more than I can deliver, Margie."

"I never thought you would," she said with a smile.

He studied her again, his gaze lingering on the bodice. "Maybe I was wrong about one thing," he murmured.

"What?" she asked.

"The padded bra," he whispered.

She ground her teeth together to keep from slapping him, but the color in her cheeks was unpreventable.

"You're outrageous!" she told him.

"Righteous indignation?" he asked mockingly. "Ruffled modesty? I thought you were a liberated woman."

"You make me feel about thirteen," she flung at him, and then felt like sinking into the floor for admitting such a thing to such a man.

"Do I really?" he taunted.

"Good night, Mr. Van Dyne," she muttered, turning.

"No parting kiss?" he asked with dark insolence.

"I'd bite you if you even tried," she growled.

One bushy eyebrow went up, along with a corner of his disciplined mouth. "What an intriguing thought. Where would you bite me?"

She knew when she was defeated. Without another word, she left the three of them on the steps and went straight into the house.

3

~~~~~~~~~~~~~~~~

"As if I'd want to kiss him," Margie muttered on her way up the stairs, oblivious to Jan's amused face behind her.

"Did he offer?" her sister asked.

Margie ignored the question. "He's arrogant and overbearing and simply maddening," she grumbled. "And I've got to be out of my mind for agreeing to this trip."

"You'll have a good time," came the soft promise. "And you'll be doing me the biggest favor you ever have."

Margie softened, turning at her bedroom door to smile at her sister. "I'm just pure marshmallow, and you know it." She laughed. "Maybe I can find ways to avoid that big steamroller if I work at it. I'll pack the typewriter and it will be an incentive for me to stay in my room and work like mad toward the deadline."

Jan looked guilty. "You don't mind keeping your infamous pen name under wraps, do you?" she asked uncertainly. "I wouldn't have asked you to do it without a good reason, and you must know I'm terribly proud of what you've accomplished. You're talented, you're famous . . . it's just that Cannon is so horribly conservative."

"I don't mind," Margie said. "It will be kind of nice to just be a person for a change. Back when I was a reporter, I was a camera and a notepad. Now I'm a book jacket. Some people just don't realize that under the glitter, I'm only an average person, doing a job I love. I'm nothing special."

"Oh yes, you are," Jan said, and hugged her. "Very, very special."

Margie muffled a giggle. "Cannon doesn't think so," she said dryly. "I thought he was going to banish Andy and me to the washroom at that restaurant."

Jan giggled with her. "Andy's full of fun, himself, and he does love to raise eyebrows. Even Cannon's."

"Speaking of convention," Margie muttered, "I think you may find that big brother isn't the stuffed shirt you imagine he is. He told me himself that the conservative image is a deliberate ploy to throw people off the track."

"And you believe him?"

The taller girl looked faintly troubled. "Yes," she

said quietly. "He's . . . unpredictable. Tonight I really understood that old saying about having a tiger by the tail."

"You're not afraid of him, are you?" Jan murmured with a smile in her voice.

"Me?" Margie drew herself up like an insulted princess and tossed her shawl over one shoulder with a flourish. I'll have you know that I got top marks in my class for fending men off. When it comes to self-defense, I am almost without equal. I shall fight them on the land, I shall fight them on the sea, I shall . . . where are you going?"

"Good night," Jan called back, heading straight for her room.

"But I was just getting to the good part!" Margie cried theatrically.

"Put it in a book—I'll read it," Jan promised, and closed her door quickly.

Margie turned and went into her bedroom with a smug grin.

But it was a long time before she slept. Her dreams, when they came, were filled with Cannon Van Dyne. She sat straight up in bed, her body on fire, her breath coming unsteadily. Her lips tingled, the way they had when his finger had parted them, teased them. He might look like a staid business executive, but he knew what to do with a woman. She would bet that there was very little he didn't know about feminine responses. And that was disquieting. She might become vulnerable to such an overwhelmingly masculine man, and she didn't want to be taken over. She'd already felt her pulse flutter wildly when he touched her. She hated the thought that he could have any power over her at all.

She was going to have to keep a safe distance from him when they got to Panama City. That would be her only hope. She couldn't risk getting involved with another Larry. She liked the taste of freedom too much.

Margie dressed in a conservative white linen suit with a pale green blouse Friday morning, and laughed when Jan came downstairs in a mint green sundress.

"Now I really feel overdressed," Margie moaned. "And I'll bet Andy will be wearing shorts, won't he?"

"No telling about Andy." The younger woman grinned. "But you look very nice."

"So do you. Well, let's doublecheck and make sure everything's turned off and locked." Margie and Jan had made all the arrangements for a two-week absence, canceling Margie's appointments, notifying Jan's boss and enlisting Mrs. James's help to watch the house and take in the mail.

By the time they'd gone over the top floor and walked back downstairs, a car was pulling up in the driveway. Margie's heart began to cartwheel. She brushed back her loosened dark hair with a hand that almost trembled with anticipation. Surely it was the thought of the plane trip, not Cannon, causing this unusual nervousness!

"They're here!" Jan laughed, running for the door. Margie couldn't remember a time in their lives when her younger sister had been so full of life and laughter. It was worth any sacrifice to see her stay that way.

Jan threw open the door, and there was Andy, dressed in Bermuda shorts, a plain tan shirt and socks and sneakers. He bent and kissed Jan gently, slowly, before he raised his head to greet Margie.

"I told you I was overdressed," Margie sighed.

"You look very elegant," Andy observed critically.

She struck a pose. "Do call *Vogue* and tell them I'm ready and willing to do their next cover, will you?"

Jan and Andy giggled, but Cannon's sudden appearance in the doorway was enough to end their merriment. He looked bone weary and not a little out of humor. He was wearing a safari suit that, on any other man, would have been pretentious. But Margie could actually picture him as the Great White Hunter in khaki tan, with a train of bearers lined up behind him and a rifle over one shoulder. An aura of adventure clung to him like cologne.

"Are we going by Capetown on the way?" Margie couldn't resist asking as Andy picked up the cases and led Jan out the door.

Cannon stared at her, his eyes hot with some violent emotion.

"Three hours and four cups of coffee from now, I might laugh at that," he told her. "But right now, I just want to get going."

"Why, honey, never let it be said that I stood in

the path of a busy man!" she drawled, grabbing her purse.

He didn't move, as she'd expected him to, and she barreled right into his big, solid body with an audible gasp.

He held her by the shoulders, looking down at her with eyes that made her flush.

"Drop the act," he said quietly. "Be yourself, with me at least."

She couldn't quite catch her breath. He made her feel funny—young and nervous. "It isn't an act," she managed shakily.

His fingers tightened and she stiffened involuntarily. "Porcelain," he murmured. "Just as beautiful and every bit as brittle. Come on, honey, I've been up half the night talking mergers, and I'm dead on my feet. Let's go."

"You're sure you're up to flying?" she asked.

"No, I'm not," he admitted surprisingly. "That's why I've had my own pilot sent out to fly us to Panama City. I've got to make half a dozen phone calls on the way, and even I can't talk and fly at the same time."

She followed along behind him, almost running to keep up. "Jan, did you get my typewriter?" she called, interrupting a lazy conversation between Andy and Jan.

"Sure did." Jan grinned. "It's in the trunk, with our bags."

"Do you need that hard-working lady writer image to impress people?" Cannon asked with a maddening, taunting smile.

"I told you, I like to keep a few articles ahead." She glanced up at him as he opened the door for her. "And look who's making cracks about hard work. Do you ever slow down?"

"In bed," he admitted.

She flushed and looked away quickly, aware of a quickening pulse.

He laughed deep in his throat. "My, what an interesting mind you have. I meant, I do sleep."

She shifted restlessly. "It's a lovely day for a trip!" she said brightly.

The Van Dyne summer home was located just a few miles outside Panama City, Florida. It was surrounded by a high, white stone wall, inside of which was a long and winding paved driveway lined with palm trees and blooming hibiscus. The house itself was also stone, spacious and venerable with mahogany doors and a curving staircase with mahogany banisters. The furniture had a West Indian look; the hall was floored with flagstone. The rest of the house was elegantly furnished and carpeted, with heavy draperies at the big windows and what-nots on shelves and tables—wickedly expensive little what-nots that most women would have given their eyeteeth for.

Victorine Van Dyne fit into her surroundings perfectly. She was like the furnishings of her summer home—elegant, venerable and charming. She resembled both her sons. Her eyes were dark brown like Cannon's, but her face was open and friendly, like Andy's. She was very petite, with a delicate bone structure and a soft, short cloud of pure silver hair framing her ageless face.

"I've heard so much about you both from Cannon and Andrew," Victorine said with a twinkle in her dark eyes. "Different versions, you understand," she added mischievously. "I had very little input from Cannon until early this week, when I got quite an earful. But I'm very pleased to meet you."

Jan impulsively hugged the smaller woman after Cannon made the introductions, and Victorine returned the embrace with slight reserve. Her attention was on Margie.

Margie smiled wickedly. "Despite what I'm sure you were told about me; I'm not a member of the world's oldest profession."

Victorine grinned at her. "I was going to ask you how you enjoyed your work." She laughed. "I guess I'd better ask what you do, first."

"She just stays at home and shocks the neighbors," Cannon said over his shoulder as he disappeared up the stairs with several suitcases. Jan and Andy followed him up, trying hard not to break into laughter.

"Now," Victorine said when they were alone. "Suppose you tell me what's been going on?"

Margie did, sparing herself nothing. "One thing led to another, and after our first meeting he was convinced that I was a madam. After the second, he wanted to put me in a day-care center. Now, I think he might like to grind me up for sausage," she added with a grin.

"Beware, my girl," the older woman warned

with a laugh. "He's never taken such a violent dislike to anyone at first sight before. It could be an omen."

Margie's eyebrows arched. "Is that anything like an incantation?"

Victorine eyed the younger woman. "Cannon said you were a widow."

"Yes, I am." She lowered her eyes. "My husband died in a plane crash five years ago."

"I lost my own husband about that long ago," Victorine sighed. "The loss was devastating not only to me, but to Cannon, because he inherited all the responsibility. Andrew does help, of course, but Cannon is the corporation."

"A man under pressure," Margie commented.

"Under a great deal of it, and he doesn't spare himself. Somewhere along the way, my eldest forgot how to play. He lost his sense of humor, too. There was a difficult marriage, and an even more difficult divorce. It was a blessing that there were no children involved." She glanced at Margie. "Did you . . . ?"

"No," she said curtly, much more curtly than she meant to.

Victorine laid a delicate hand on her forearm. "Not a happy marriage?" she asked softly.

Margie shook her head, and for just an instant the mask slipped.

The older woman, in that instant, seemed to see it all. She turned away. "Let's sit down and get acquainted. I have angina pectoris, and I find it difficult to move around too much, although I try." She looked angry for a second. "I'm protected to death, you know. Cannon has the employees spy on me."

Margie's eyes brightened. "He what?"

Victorine frowned as she sat down on the sofa beside Margie. "He has me spied on, and if I do things he and that idiotic doctor say I shouldn't, he gets furious."

"You do have your trials, I can see that," Margie said. "Having to live with him must be the biggest of all."

Victorine smiled. She was going to enjoy this young woman. And she had a strange feeling that Cannon might eventually share that view.

The days passed lazily, with Cannon usually off on business meetings. Jan and Margie settled in, enjoying the sun and sand, talking to Victorine, watching television and enjoying the French cook's delicious fare. It was the kind of break Margie had needed for a long time, and she found herself relaxing, taking things easy. She worked on the book at a leisurely pace, mostly early in the morning so she wouldn't disturb the household.

But always, she was aware of Cannon's speculative gaze when he was in the house. He watched her the way a cat watches its prey, with a narrow, unblinking gaze that made her nervous.

"Are you looking for warts?" she asked him on their third day at the beach house while waiting for the others to sit down to dinner.

"Would I find any?" he asked lazily, leaning back in the big armchair that seemed to be his personal property.

"Not where they show," she mused.

"Now you've intrigued me," he replied, and his dark eyes did a slow, bold survey of her body. She was wearing a strappy little white dress and suddenly her body felt as if someone had stroked it.

She wished she could give him the same kind of sensual appraisal, but she wouldn't have dared. He was wearing a blue silk shirt, open halfway down the chest, with white slacks, and he looked good enough to star in any motion picture.

"I'm having a group of men here tomorrow night for dinner and a business discussion," he said out of the blue, pausing to light a cigarette and take a draw from it before he went on. "I'd appreciate it if you didn't hang from the chandelier or wear a backless gown."

"I don't own a backless gown," she informed him.

One corner of his mouth curled up. "Not even to shock Mrs. James?" he taunted.

"I have to draw the line somewhere," she said defensively.

He watched her hands pleat the wispy fabric of her skirt. "I like your hair loose like that," he remarked, letting his eyes lift to the long, deliciously disheveled length of it. "It's sexy."

She colored and all but jumped to her feet. "Shouldn't we go on in?" she asked.

He got up too, lazily, dangerously, and moved toward her like a jungle cat, with a grace of movement that was peculiarly his own.

"You're afraid of me," he said as he approached her. "Why?"

She backed away with a laughing shrug. "Not afraid, just wary. You make me feel hemmed in sometimes."

"Do I?" he mused, watching her from his superior height. "What an interesting reaction."

She glared at him. "I thought you had a meeting somewhere tonight."

He chuckled deeply. "Trying to get rid of me, Margie? Yes, I do have a meeting, but not until after dinner."

"Business seems to take up most of your life," she remarked quietly.

He nodded, lifting the cigarette to his wide, chiseled lips. He was watching her, classifying her, and it made her shaky. "The universal panacea, Margie," he returned.

"Do you need one?" she blurted out.

He searched her wide eyes. "Do you?" he asked. "You spend a great deal of time at that typewriter for someone just doing the occasional article. Does it compensate?"

"For what?" she asked, resisting the urge to move away.

"For a lover," he said bluntly, and smiled mockingly as the shock registered in her green eyes.

4

~~~~~~~~~~~~~~~

She felt her breath stop momentarily as she looked up into his dark, laughing eyes.

"I don't want a lover," she said coldly.

"You make that quite obvious. But you need one," he said, unabashed. "You look like a woman who hasn't been touched in years. Or stroked," he murmured, reaching out to run his fingers down her cheek.

She jerked wildly away from him, her eyes dilating, her mouth parted. "Don't . . . !" she warned.

He lifted his dark head and studied her with narrowed eyes, the cigarette making a tiny smoke-screen between them. "You don't like to be touched, do you?" he asked. "Which only goes to prove my point. How long has it been since a man kissed you—really kissed you, with passion?"

She felt as if she were choking. "Sex isn't everything, Mr. Van Dyne," she ground out.

"Spoken like a nun," he applauded.

She lashed out at him. "That's all you men ever think about," she accused. "What do you care about a woman's needs?"

"What do you know about a woman's needs?" he challenged. His eyes wandered over her taut body. "Tell me something, Silver. Did your husband really die in a plane crash, or did he freeze to death in your bed?"

She lifted her hand automatically, an involuntary response, a purely passionate act. But he was fast. He caught her wrist in a grip like steel and halted her fingers just inches from his tanned cheek.

"Lift your hand to me again, wildcat, and I'll throw you down on the floor and teach you lessons in passion you've never learned," he warned softly.

"What would you know about passion, you walking business machine?" she threw back, her hair wild as she struggled to free herself, her face alive and desperately beautiful.

He laughed softly. One big arm shot out to catch her and drag her against his taut body, holding her there with effortless ease.

She looked up at him with frightened eyes, her struggles intensifying, her face mirroring the apprehension she was feeling.

"Damn you," she breathed, trying to kick his shins.

"Finally," he murmured. "The real woman, under the facade."

She pushed at his massive chest and her hands came in contact with his muscles under their covering of curling, crisp hair. She froze at the unfamiliar contact. She had always avoided touching Larry. But her hands liked the feel of Cannon's flesh, and because of that, she dragged her fingers away as if they'd been burned.

He caught a handful of her silky hair and held her head where he wanted it. His eyes had gone darker while she fought him, until now they were almost black, and there was no smile in them. His gaze dropped to her soft, parted lips and his nostrils flared.

"Let me go, Cannon," she whispered shakily.

"We fought, honey," he replied in a husky, deep tone. "And you lost. Haven't you ever heard to whom the spoils belong?"

His head was already moving down, and she was afraid of him, afraid of being forced into submission.

"Oh, please, no . . . !" she cried, her face going white as she saw Larry's face above her, insensitive, intent with sexual need. . . .

Cannon was supporting her weight suddenly, lifting her all at once to carry her to the sofa and hover over her with puzzled, concerned eyes.

"Want a brandy?" he asked softly.

She shook her head, drawing in quick breaths. She closed her eyes, hoping he'd go away.

"Then will you tell me what the hell is the matter

with you?" he asked shortly. "I move toward you and you back away. I touch you, and you look as if I've stripped off your skin. And just now . . . my God, did you think I was going to rape you?"

She couldn't look at him. "I don't like being held against my will," she breathed. "I can't bear it."

"So I've noticed."

"Then why do it?" she blazed, her voice breaking.

He drew in a harsh breath. "You chip at my pride," he ground out. "I don't like being told I'm a walking business machine with no feelings."

She sat up and sighed wearily. "It isn't you," she said in a fatigued tone. "Not you at all."

"Then what?" he demanded.

She laughed bitterly. "Stop trying to storm the gates, will you, Attila the Hun?" she asked. "I don't pry into your life, do I?"

He scowled darkly. "No, you don't. And that irritates me just as much," he murmured as he turned to watch the others saunter in, oblivious to the tension in the air.

"Saved!" she whispered to irritate him.

"Only for the moment," he promised.

Margie was just about to go up to bed later that evening when Cannon returned from his business meeting. He went to the padded bar and poured himself a brandy, hardly sparing her a glance. His shirt was still undone almost to the waist and he had a white jacket slung over one shoulder. He threw the jacket onto the bar stool and tossed back the drink. His dark hair was ruffled, as if by the sea breeze, and his eyes were bloodshot and shadowed with fatigue.

Margie edged away, hoping to make her escape without speaking to him, but Cannon moved between her and the door with a smile so mocking that she seated herself on the couch instead.

"What is it about me that gives you these impulses to turn around and run?" he asked curtly, dropping down on the sofa beside her and crossing his powerful legs.

"I don't like your approach," she threw back, rubbing her upper arms.

"My God, what approach?" he growled. "You started to hit me, remember?"

Her face went cold. "And do you remember what you said to me?"

"Not all of it," he admitted. "It wasn't important enough." He took a deep breath while she fumed silently. "God, I'm tired. The older I get, the more I'm convinced that lower-level executives were created to drive men mad."

"You've been dealing with one, I gather?" she asked, clenching her hands in her lap. She wasn't about to run from him.

He laughed shortly. "That's a pleasant way of putting it."

Her eyes fell on his well-shaped hand holding the cigarette he was smoking. He had strong hands, she thought, very masculine hands. Her eyes involuntarily lifted to his broad, half-bare chest, and she felt a tremor go through her body as she remembered the feel of it under her hands. She hadn't meant to touch him, she hadn't wanted to, but that fleeting contact with his hair-roughened flesh had done incredible things to her. Embarrassed at her own thoughts, she dropped her eyes back to his hands and felt her cheeks coloring.

"Do my hands embarrass you?" he asked quietly. "I can always stick them in my pockets."

She cleared her throat. "I was thinking of something," she mumbled.

He finished the cigarette and crushed it out in the ashtray beside him. "You don't drink, do you?" he asked conversationally. "You never touched your drink at Louis Dane's, and you always leave your wine untouched at meals."

She glanced up at him. "I don't like alcohol," she admitted. "You'll never know the names I called you when you ordered me that drink I didn't touch the first night we met—and left me stuck with the bill."

He chuckled delightedly. "I'll make amends one of these days." He leaned a long, powerful arm across the back of the sofa and studied her, the action widening the gap of his shirt so that Margie had to look away or be hypnotized by the blatant masculinity of his bareness. "Why don't you drink?"

"I can't get the stuff past my nose," she told him.

"Is that the truth? Or is alcohol attached to some unpleasant memory in your past?"

She thought of her father's alcoholism and felt herself turn pale. "I like your mother very much," she said, changing the subject. "She's a character."

He hesitated before he let her change the subject. "She had to be," he said after a minute. "My father was a retired army colonel who saw service in two wars. He was miserable in peacetime and amused himself by regimenting the people around him."

"Especially you?" she probed softly.

He cocked an eyebrow. "Perceptive, aren't you?" He chuckled. "Yes, especially me. At least until I outgrew my adolescent yearning for his praise. We fought like hell until he died—and he loved every minute of it."

She searched his dark eyes. "And Andy?"

He shrugged. "Andy fights no one, least of all me," he added challengingly.

"Is that a warning?" she asked.

"You might take it as one." He lit a cigarette without offering her one. "Andy isn't strong willed. He needs a woman sophisticated enough to keep the wolves at bay."

"You're insinuating that he's a weakling who needs a built-in battle axe," she shot back. "That's insulting and it's untrue. Andy may be full of fun, but he's no marshmallow. You may find that out someday."

He lifted both eyebrows insolently. "Are you presuming to describe my brother to me?"

"Just because you've lived with him, don't sit there so smugly and assume that you know him like the back of your hand," she returned sharply. "You never really know other people. We all have a deeply private side that even our closest kin don't see."

"Then how do you know about Andy's other side?" he taunted.

"I learned to read people when I worked on the newspaper staff," she informed him. "Andy's got a lot of steel under that easy friendliness. You just haven't discovered it because he's never wanted anything before that you told him he couldn't have. Tell him he can't have Jan and watch what happens," she challenged.

His dark eyes narrowed menacingly, and the forgotten cigarette sent curls of gray smoke into the air between them.

"My God, you've got nerve."

"What's wrong, Mr. Van Dyne," she chided, "aren't you used to people talking back to you?"

"No," he admitted.

"Well, you may intimidate your board of directors, but it's going to take a lot more than an underwear manufacturer . . . oh!"

She gasped as his hand shot out and caught her by the nape of the neck, jerking her face under his.

"Keep pushing," he said under his breath. "I'm tired and out of humor, and you've already gotten under my skin once this evening."

"Let go!" she ground out, pushing furiously at his chest, as she had earlier in the evening when she'd fought and lost. But now there was something different—her excited pulses were racing, but not out of fear.

His hand contracted, forcing her cheek onto his shoulder. He didn't touch her in any other way, only with that relentless hand as inflexible as steel.

"Go ahead, honey, fight me," he murmured, holding her gaze as his head started to bend. "But the only thing you're going to accomplish by twisting your body against mine is to arouse me even more. . . ."

She caught her breath at the suggestive remark, and while her lips were parted, he took them.

She felt her body freeze in a shocked arch as his warm, hard lips crushed down on her mouth, his teeth faintly bruising against the soft flesh. She breathed in the smoky, brandied taste of him, the aura of expensive cologne, and felt a strange new emotion burning at the ice around her body. He was incredibly strong, his hand holding her neck still, his mouth deliberately insulting, his tongue doing things to her that made her blush. She could have gone for him with her long nails, but she didn't. They were clenched at her own chest, locked there.

She groaned, opening her eyes to find him looking back at her, amused mockery in his gaze as his mouth controlled and dominated hers.

It was the most sensuous thing she could ever have imagined. Never before had a man looked into her eyes while he kissed her, and a surge of the most unbelievable warmth shot through her. That frightened her more than his strength did. Suddenly she tore her mouth away from his and ducked, escaping his hand. Her movement was so quick that she lost her balance and fell backwards, catching the sofa arm to halt her descent. She was breathing hard, her eyes wild with fear and outrage and excitement, her lips bruised, her body trembling. She looked at him like an animal at bay.

He watched her narrowly, not a hair out of place as he lifted the cigarette to his mouth with steady fingers.

"That was disgusting," she bit off, her eyes accusing, glittering.

A shadow clouded his eyes, but his bland expression didn't change. "You asked for it, honey," he replied casually.

"Not me, mister," she returned, fighting to catch her breath. "I don't get my kicks by being mauled."

He frowned slightly. "Is that what you call a kiss, Silver—being mauled?"

She stood up and moved away, her knees slightly weak, her mind whirling with confusion. How could she tell him, make him understand how deep the scars from her marriage went? He'd never understand, anyway. Not a male chauvinist like him!

"I'm going to bed," she choked, licking her dry lips to find the taste of him still on them.

"Running from the enemy?" he taunted.

She turned with her hand on the doorknob, gloriously beautiful in her fury, her green eyes like Colombian emeralds sparkling in the sun. "God only knows what you're capable of," she flung at him.

He leaned back against the sofa, his eyes insolently appraising. "Well, don't get your hopes up, honey," he murmured. "I have to toss the women out of my bedroom as it is. You'd have to wait in line for the chance."

"I wouldn't even buy a ticket," she assured him.

"That works both ways," he returned. He laughed bitterly. "It was like making love to a corpse."

She caught her breath. That hurt. It actually hurt. She turned, opening the door.

"Margie!" he called suddenly.

She paused for an instant, with her back to him, then rushed into the hall and slammed the door behind her. She didn't stop running until she got to her room.

5

∿∿∿∿∿∿∿∿∿∿

Margie and Cannon barely spoke at the breakfast table, and she avoided his gaze completely. She couldn't bear the mocking amusement she knew she'd find there, the memory of his kiss was still too fresh.

"What time are your guests coming, dear?" Victorine asked Cannon as they finished breakfast and settled back with a second cup of coffee.

"At six," he replied, and Margie felt his eyes on her. "I meant what I said about clothes, Mrs. Silver. If you come down those stairs in anything shocking, I'll carry you back up them myself."

Margie didn't reply. She kept her eyes doggedly on her plate and listened while his chair scraped as he stood up. Then there was a muffled sound followed by footsteps dying away.

"Well," Victorine murmured, watching Margie. "What was that all about? Did you two have a falling out?"

Margie lifted her eyes, grateful that Jan and Andy hadn't been around to witness the scene. "You might call it that," she murmured curtly. She sipped her coffee. "He's just insufferable!"

"So was his father," Victorine volunteered. She smiled wistfully. "But I loved the old devil to distraction. I found quite by accident that when he was the most furious and intimidating, I could calm him right down just by putting my arms around him."

Margie stared at her. "I'd rather be shot than put my arms around Cannon."

The older woman grinned. "Would you, really? Or does he disturb you, my dear?"

She shifted nervously. "He . . . frightens me."

"Yes, I know. You frighten him, too. He's never been so hostile to a guest before. I can see him bristle when you walk into a room, and his eyes follow you everywhere."

Margie looked hunted. She reached for her coffee cup too quickly and almost upset it, then caught her breath sharply as she righted it again.

Victorine placed a gentle hand over hers. "Don't be intimidated by him, Margie. He's tough, because he's always had to be. But one thing I can promise you, he'd never deliberately hurt you."

She almost disputed that, until she realized she *had* provoked him into that violent confrontation. And then she began to wonder why. Had she known, even then, that if she made him angry enough, he'd touch her? Had she wanted him to?

"He's a very lonely man," the older woman continued.

"That isn't what he told me," she muttered, her eyes narrowing. "He said he had to shake the women out of his bed." She remembered to whom she was talking and flushed.

Victorine grinned delightedly. "Now I wonder why he said such a thing?" she murmured. "And it's not true. Since Della left him—rather since he threw her out—he's had no deep involvement with any woman. Oh, there are the glittery women that he's sometimes seen with. He's a man, after all, my dear. But he's kept his heart quite deliberately tucked away, out of reach. And he hasn't allowed anyone close enough to touch it."

Margie studied the black liquid in her cup with a preoccupied stare. "May I ask you why his wife . . . ran around?"

Victorine smiled wistfully. "Not for the reason you might think," she said gently. "Della simply liked men—I think there's a medical term for that kind of obsession with sex. Cannon's pride took quite a blow before he finally got tired enough of it to do something decisive." She studied the younger woman intensely. "Your husband was cruel to you in bed, wasn't he?" she asked quietly, and sighed. "Oh, my dear, all marriages aren't like that. You had a bad experience, but I'm afraid you're letting it ruin the rest of your life. You mustn't, Margie." She reached over and touched Margie's hand lightly. "You're much too young to stop living."

Margie's wide eyes found the older woman's and all her fears were revealed in them. "The men in my life haven't been the cream of the crop," she said quietly. "What I knew of my own father was terribly unpleasant, and my husband was just another disappointment. . . ." She looked up. "I suppose all men aren't monsters, but how do you tell the good guys from the bad guys before you've lived with them?" she murmured wistfully. "I thought Larry was the best in the world. If I couldn't trust my judgment then, how can I ever trust it again?"

Victorine looked troubled. "You have to learn to trust again," she said. "I realize that's easier said than done, but you may find that it comes naturally when you meet the right man."

The younger woman sighed, finishing her coffee. She smiled shyly. "I've never talked to anyone like this. Except possibly Jan."

"Then I'm flattered. What about your mother?"

"She died when Jan was born. I barely remember her. We were raised by our grandmother McPherson, a fierce old lady who was more interested in discipline than affection." She sighed, smiling. "We loved her, but we grew up with only each other."

Victorine was watching her with a strange expression on her face, watchful, calculating. "McPherson?" she murmured.

Margie could have bitten her tongue out. Had

Victorine solved the puzzle? Was her identity about to be exposed?

"Is something wrong?" she asked, studying the older woman.

Victorine shrugged. "I keep thinking I've heard that name somewhere." She laughed. "And you looked so familiar . . . oh, well, I suppose we all have counterparts, don't we?"

"Yes, I suppose we do," came the relieved reply.

"I like your sister," Victorine said quietly. "I like the way my youngest acts around her. So protective and capable—so different from my old Andy, who was forever hoping for Cannon's approval. He's changing right before my eyes."

"Jan loves him very much," Margie remarked. "She's happy in a way she's never been. Poor little Jan. She was always on the receiving end of Larry's temper, but she had to stay with us because she had no place else to go. Now that Andy's come into her life, she smiles and plays . . . I thought she'd forgotten how."

The older woman looked thoughtful. "Doesn't that apply to you, too?" she asked gently. "I hear that typewriter all hours of the day. Are you another of those frustrated would-be novelists, Margie, out to write the Great American Novel? Come on, 'fess up. Are you?"

Margie burst into gales of laughter. "All right, yes, I am."

"I knew it! What kind of books do you try to write—those delicious mystery novels?"

"Yes," Margie lied, "however did you guess?"

The older woman laughed. "I don't know, it just popped into my mind. Now, personally, I like those huge sexy historical novels. I read them by the dozen." Her eyes were speculative as she studied Margie's face. "Do you read those?"

"Oh no, they're much too suggestive for my taste," Margie lied again and prayed silently for forgiveness.

"I see." Victorine lowered her eyes to her coffee, but there was a strange, tiny little smile on her mouth.

"Cannon doesn't want Jan and Andy to marry," Margie said, missing that giveaway smile.

"Yes, I know." Victorine finished her coffee. "But he'll get over it. All he needs is to be around Jan for awhile, see her with Andy and get to know her. He's simply against marriage. He's very protective of Andy and he doesn't want him to make a mistake. Cannon's marriage made him bitter—very much as yours made you bitter, I imagine. But he'll come around."

Margie sighed. "Oh, I hope you're right. I do hope you are."

Margie had hoped that she could stay in her room that night to escape the guests who were coming to see Cannon—as well as to avoid the man himself. She didn't want another confrontation with him until she sorted her feelings out. But Victorine wouldn't hear of it.

"You most certainly will not hide in your room," the older woman said, her small figure drawn up to its full height.

"Oh, it wouldn't be hiding," Margie promised. "I'd just sort of hibernate for the night and hoard my strength for tomorrow."

"No," Victorine said firmly. "And wear something shocking," she added with a grin. "So will I. We'll show him!"

Margie burst out laughing. "You'll be the greatest mother-in-law. . . ."

"I don't suppose you'd care to apply for the position of my daughter-in-law?" Victorine asked hopefully.

"Andy wants Jan."

"You know very well I didn't mean Andy." She cocked her head in the same way Cal did. "He wants you, you know. It's written all over him."

Margie's eyes fell. "I don't want that kind of involvement. I'm afraid."

"So is he," she replied, and smiled at Margie's incredulous expression. "It's true. Della soured him. He's made sure that his women friends are very sophisticated and freedom loving—and that their idea of commitment is a hotel room rented for one night," she added wickedly.

"Which is about all he wants with me," Margie said quietly.

"Are you very sure of that?" Victorine asked. "You might be surprised, my dear. Now hurry and dress. And don't forget—shocking apparel!"

But as it was, Margie was out of shocking clothes, having left all her daring gowns back in Georgia. Instead, she followed her mood and chose a gauzy Victorian-style dress with a high collar and a lacy insert above the ruffled bodice, and a flaring skirt boasting a ruffle around the bottom. With it, she put on lace-up high heels that flattered her small feet. She piled her dark hair into a high coiffure and used the lightest touch of makeup. The result was sheer elegance, an illusion of old-fashioned delicacy that suited her slender figure and matched her reserved mood.

She went downstairs alone, meeting Victorine and Jan at the bottom of the stairs.

"This is shocking?" the older woman asked, shifting to emphasize her deeply plunging, plum velvet gown as she glared at Margie's outfit.

"It shows my ankles," Margie explained, nodding toward them. "At the turn of the century, that was quite shocking."

Victorine laughed delightedly. "So it was."

Margie studied Jan, delightful in the silky pale yellow gown that clung to the soft lines of her figure.

"You look like a tea rose," she told her younger sister.

"Doesn't she, though?" Victorine agreed, surveying her. "Superb taste in clothes, my dear. It will matter, one of these days."

Jan colored prettily and smiled. "I didn't want to embarrass Andy by coming down in something flamboyant."

"What's this?" Andy asked, moving toward them in his elegant evening clothes. "Embarrass me? Like fun."

Jan laughed delightedly, running to him. "Do I look all right?" she asked, wanting his approval.

"Good enough to eat," he murmured, bending to brush a kiss across her forehead.

"Could you save that for the bedroom?" Cannon growled, joining them, his eyes intimidating as they met his brother's. "I can't walk through the house without finding you two in a clinch somewhere."

"Don't look, if it bothers you, brother dear," Andy said with a sudden, uncharacteristic show of spirit. Then he smiled coolly. "And for your information, Jan and I aren't sharing a bedroom. There'll be plenty of time for that—after we marry."

"Without my approval?" Cannon asked insolently.

Andy straightened, drawing Jan closer. "If we have to, yes. Take a look, Cal. I'm all grown up now. I'm not the high school kid who used to worship at the altar of your machismo. And whether you believe it or not, I'm quite capable of supporting Jan and myself."

"Working at what, exactly?" Cannon asked.

Andy shifted. "At the mill, of course."

"Think again," Cannon replied, his eyes glittering with triumph. "If you marry without my consent, you'll start from scratch and without a penny."

"Cannon . . . !" Victorine began.

"The trust is set up so that I have full control over your purse strings until you attain the ripe old age of thirty," Cannon added, ramming a hand in his pocket to draw out his cigarette case. "And there's no question about my authority to hire and fire as I please. So don't throw your weight around with me, boy. It will get you exactly nowhere."

"If you'll excuse us," Andy said quietly to Victorine and Margie, "I think we'll spend the evening in town."

Jan looked close to tears, and Margie's heart went out to her. Damn Cannon! As she was thinking it, her eyes were telling him how she felt. But he didn't even flinch.

"I'm so sorry we have guests coming," Victorine told her eldest son with blazing eyes and a cold smile. "I'd love to discuss that little speech with you, dear boy."

He smiled in amusement at his mother's bridled fury. "No doubt you would, Mother dear. But despite the pressure from you and Andy, I'm not budging one inch until I'm convinced that he isn't making a mistake in his choice."

"Will you spend the rest of his life telling him which women to date, which fork to use, which television programs he may watch . . . ?" Margie broke in.

"It's none of your business," he replied curtly.

"Jan is my sister; of course it's my business." She glared at him. "She's had quite enough heartache in her life without having to be barbequed by an overprotective stuffed shirt like you!"

Cannon looked as if he'd like to take a bite out of her, and Victorine had just opened her mouth to speak when the doorbell sounded.

"Oh, your guests are here," Victorine said quickly. "The maid will let them in, but shouldn't we greet them?"

Cannon was still glaring at Margie. "Later," he said menacingly, "you and I are going to have a few words together."

"Oh, I'll just look *forward* to it!" Margie drawled, smiling sweetly.

He turned and strode angrily toward the front door while Victorine gave a mock sigh of relief, drawing Margie along with her.

There were two businessmen at the door, one tall and solemn, one short and heavyset with a red face. Cannon followed them into the living room, sparing Margie a pointed glare as he introduced Bob Long and Harry Neal.

In short order, Margie found herself standing alone with Bob Long as the others argued about the current administration's economic policies.

"Do you argue politics, Mr. Long?" Margie asked politely.

He shook his head, looking somewhat irritated. "My great interest is water conservation." He glanced at her. "And I'd hardly expect you to know much about that."

His chauvinistic attitude pricked her a little, but she smiled. "On the contrary, Mr. Long, it's an interest of mine, as well. I come from a small town outside Atlanta. We use two million gallons of water per day, and we draw from a tributary of the Chattahoochee River. The nearest town to us has a processing plant that uses a million gallons a day on its own, to say nothing of the city's consumption of three million gallons a day."

Bob Long stared at her as if he feared his hearing had failed him. "And it draws from the same tributary?"

"Partially," she said. "But last year, when the drought came, the town had to drill three additional wells to meet water consumption, and right now we're looking at the feasibility of a countywide water and sewage system."

"That's just what happened to us," he replied, and proceeded to tell her how the problem had come about and what the governing body had done to alleviate it.

They were busily discussing new legislation allocating water consumption by municipalities when Cannon interrupted them.

"I hate to break this up, Bob," he murmured with a hard glance at Margie, "but Harry and I need some input from you on the merger proposal."

"Merger." Bob Long blinked. "Oh, yes, the merger." He turned and shook hands with Margie. "I can't remember when I've enjoyed a conversation so much. We must do this again."

Cannon gave her a strange, puzzled glance as he led the older man away.

Andy and Jan had just rejoined the group. Andy looking fighting fit, and Jan herself looked as if she were ready to enter into the fray with her man. Even Cannon's harsh look when they came into the room wasn't enough to bother either of them.

"Well, well," Margie teased. "Changed your minds?"

"Sure did." Andy grinned. "I took a course in advanced dragon slaying in college. I went outside, looked at the car and decided that running is something you only do when the odds are stacked against you."

"Same here," Jan said with a rare show of spirit. "Cannon may not like me, but by gosh, he's going to accept me one of these days."

Margie grinned at them. "That's the spirit. I'll help any way I can, right down to supporting the two of you while you get started if it comes to that."

Andy gave her a warm smile. "I wouldn't let you do that," he said gently. "But having your support means a lot. Thanks."

"What are future sisters-in-law for?" Margie shrugged theatrically.

"By the way," Andy asked, "was old man Long actually smiling at you when we came in? He hates people. Mostly he stands in corners and sneers into his drink until it's time to talk business, and then he disagrees with everything that's been said."

"That name sounds familiar," Jan murmured.

"It ought to—I've been moaning over it for weeks." He glanced at Margie. "Cal's trying to talk Long into merging his knitting mill with our corporation. Long won't budge. They've had meeting after meeting after meeting, and Cal's had to do all the negotiating himself—but with every junior executive in Long's company. This is the first time Long's even agreed to meet with him face to face."

"I think I'm flattered," Margie murmured with a smile.

At dinner, she wasn't surprised to find herself seated next to Bob Long, who turned out to be a former planning commission member. They didn't run out of subjects all through the meal. In fact, Bob Long was the last to leave—a totally different man from the sour-faced executive of a few hours before.

"You still haven't given me an answer on the merger proposal, Bob," Cannon reminded him with a hard glance in Margie's direction.

"Oh, that." Bob waved airily. "Go ahead with it. You have your people draw up the contracts and send them over. I'll sign them. It's been a pleasure, Mrs. Silver," he added, holding Margie's slender hand in his bony one and smiling down at her. "I hope we'll meet again sometime."

"So do I, Mr. Long," she said with a genuine smile of her own. "Good night."

He nodded, waving at the others, and went smiling out the door.

"My God," Cannon said shortly, staring at Margie with glittering eyes. "I've been trying for months to get him to agree to the damned thing so that Harry and I could go ahead with our expansion plans. He wouldn't budge. He wouldn't even meet with us. And he spends a couple of hours talking to you and acts as if he couldn't care less about the whole thing!"

"He's an introvert," Margie told him. "He doesn't mix well, and that makes him argumentative. He only wants to be treated like everyone else, to be part of the conversation, but he doesn't know how."

"You did," Cannon pointed out.

"I was a reporter," she reminded him. "An old

editor told me years ago that there are no dull people—only interviewers with no imagination. After that, I went the extra mile to draw people out. It's not hard. You simply find things they like to talk about, and listen as much as you talk."

"How simple you make it sound, dear," Victorine said. "It isn't, you know."

"Anyway, I enjoyed it," Margie said. "We had quite a talk about water usage and restrictions. . . ."

"Both my sons sat on committees dealing with conservation issues in Chicago," Victorine remarked. "Cannon went on television about it."

"I didn't know Bob was even interested in water conservation," Cannon muttered, and looked at Margie as if that were her fault.

"I think we'll go watch television," Andy said, holding Jan's hand tightly and smiling down at her.

"Well, don't sit too close," Cannon warned with a faint smile. "To the set, I mean. You know what they say about radiation."

Andy managed to smile back. "So they do. But I can take care of myself, big brother. And of Jan, if she'll let me."

Cannon studied the younger man. "We'll do some serious talking one of these days."

Andy nodded. "I think we'll have to."

"I'm going for a drive," Cannon said, turning. "Get a wrap and come with me, Margie."

She glared up at him. "Not me," she replied.

"Yes you. I'll take you for a romantic ride in the moonlight," he chided.

She studied his hard face and sighed. Well, it was

inevitable that she was going to have to stand up to him. It might as well be tonight—then she wouldn't have to spend the rest of her vacation wondering when it would come.

"If I'm not back in two hours," Margie told Victorine in a stage whisper, "call the sheriff and tell him you suspect foul play."

Victorine laughed at her. "I will, but I'll do my best to protect you, dear. I'll swear he drove you to it. . . ."

"I must be out of my mind to go off with you," Margie told him once they were on the road.

"Especially at night," he agreed. "So why did you?"

She stared down at her lap, where the neon lights from signs along the highway made colorful patterns. "I don't know. I could have cheerfully choked you earlier."

"You fight for your sister, honey. Don't expect me to do less for my brother."

She turned her attention to the whitecaps that were just visible behind the rows of motels, crashing on the wet beach. "In other words, it's all in the point of view?"

"Exactly."

"Where are we going?" she asked.

He glanced at her. "That question has a familiar ring. Do you always suspect me of evil motives when I get into a car with you?"

She laughed. "Is that how I sounded? I was just curious."

"Don't worry," he said, executing a turn that led them onto a long stretch of road paralleling the beach. "I won't try to stop at any motels."

Her cheeks went hot. "I wasn't expecting you to."

"No?" He glanced her way. "Most of the time you act as if I were an escaped rapist."

"You told me yourself that you weren't a gentle man," she said, clenching her fingers together in her lap.

He glanced sideways. "The word I used was lover," he reminded her. "And I think you may have misunderstood me. I meant that I was demanding in bed, not cruel."

She felt her face burn, but she knew the dim light wasn't going to reveal that.

"No comment?" he asked. He let up on the accelerator while he took a cigarette from his pocket and lit it.

"I'm nursing my bruises," she murmured.

"You wouldn't have any if you hadn't tried to break my jaw," he reminded her.

"Well, you insulted me!" she accused.

"And just what the hell were you doing to me?" he returned. "I wouldn't presume to brag, but my God, it's been twenty years since I had to fight for a kiss from any woman—and it's never been called 'disgusting.'"

She began to understand his attitude, and felt a little ashamed of herself. He was a proud man, and her description of that kiss must have hurt something vulnerable in him. She'd been afraid, and nervous of liking it too much, but in no way had he disgusted her. She began to wonder if he ever could.

"I shouldn't have said that," she admitted quietly. "It wasn't true."

He took a long draw from the cigarette. "I'm not usually rough with women," he said after a minute. "I've never forced one. Damn it, it's the way you react to me," he added gruffly. "I can't get near you."

"And I've told you already, it's nothing personal," she threw back. She sighed, wrapping her arms around herself. "I don't enjoy sex," she confessed quietly. "It's something I can't help, so please just accept it and don't . . . don't push."

He pulled the car off the road onto a small paved area with picnic tables overlooking a stretch of sand dunes and scrub grass and diamond-sparkled water with whitecaps crashing down on the beach. He cut the engine and turned to her, his face shadowy in the moonlit confines of the car, his eyes glittering above the orange tip of his cigarette.

"Women aren't frigid unless some man makes them that way," he said shortly.

She looked down at the paleness of her skirt under her fingers. "What do you want from me, a confession?" She laughed nervously. "I'm sorry, I told you once, I'm a very private person."

"That makes two of us." He took a long draw from the cigarette. "Why do I frighten you?"

She tucked a fold into her skirt. "You're very big," she murmured.

His mouth curved slightly. "What do you want, a

man half your size so that you can beat him in hand-to-hand?" he teased.

It sounded so absurd that she laughed involuntarily. "No, I don't suppose so."

He took another draw from the cigarette and leaned forward to crush it out in the ashtray, an action that brought him close—so close that she could feel the warmth of his body, smell the intoxicating fragrance of his very masculine cologne.

He turned suddenly, so that his face was only inches away from hers, and her heart pounded wildly.

"You let me hold you once, do you remember?" he asked softly, searching her wide eyes. "I made you angry and you cried, the night we went out with Andy and Jan."

She licked her dry lips, hypnotized by his gaze. "I wanted to hit you," she recalled.

"I've noticed that's becoming a habit with you," he murmured with a smile. His hands caught her shoulders, very gently, and tugged until her resistance lessened enough to let him ease her against his body.

"Here," he breathed, sliding his arms slowly around her, giving her time to pull away if she wanted to. "Just like this, Margie, no threats, no demands. I just want to hold you."

She felt his cheek rough against hers, felt the slow, steady rhythm of his breathing against her soft breasts, which were pressed gently against his broad chest. He wasn't forcing her or overpowering her, and she knew that if she struggled the least bit, he'd let her go. The knowledge reassured her, and she relaxed, letting her hands rest gently on his shoulders.

"You see?" he murmured, his voice as deep and soothing as the sound of the waves on the beach. "I won't hurt you."

Her eyes closed, and she let him take her full weight, for the first time giving in without a fight. It was odd, the sensations this kind of yielding caused in her slender body: a tingling, a muffled excitement heightening her senses, making her aware of his warmth, his powerful body, the scent of him, the hard strength of his hands pressing lightly against her back through the whisper-thin fabric of her dress.

She felt him shift, easing her closer so that she was lying across his broad thighs with her head falling naturally onto his shoulder. She watched him as he watched her, his eyes wandering quietly over every visible inch of her.

"It's like holding a tiny wild thing," he murmured softly. His hand came up to brush the wisps of unruly hair away from her flushed cheeks. "You're very soft, Margie. Skin like silk to touch."

Her fingers touched his mouth hesitantly, feeling the hard warmth of it, tracing it. They touched his square jaw, his cheek, the roughness where his skin was shadowed with a day's growth of beard. She liked the feel of him. It was the first time since her marriage that she'd wanted to touch a man.

His nose rubbed lightly, sensuously, against hers. "Kiss me, Margie," he coaxed, his mouth poised just over hers, almost but not quite touching, taunting, tormenting.

Her fingers stilled on his cheek. "You could make me," she whispered nervously, feeling her ground.

"Isn't that what's wrong with you now, honey?" he asked. "Too much 'making?' I'm not going to force you. If you want my mouth, take it."

Her hands moved over his jacket and she looked up at him, dazed, feeling the hard, heavy beat of his heart at her fingertips. Experimentally, she touched her lips to his. Once. Twice. She kissed him with a teasing pressure that left her unsatisfied, and still he didn't move.

Confident now, she slid her hands up into the thick, cool strands of hair at the back of his head and lifted her body against his. She felt her breasts crushed softly against his shirt front as she put her lips slowly over his mouth; her eyes looked straight into his the whole time. Her mouth opened, coaxing him to do the same, so that she could taste his smoky flavor. His eyes were open too, watching her responses when his tongue flicked sensually at her parted lips, teasing the inner softness with maddening expertise.

She caught her breath at the new sensations he was making her feel.

His lips still touched hers when he spoke. "It shocked you that night, didn't it?" he murmured. "Watching each other while we kissed."

"I never had," she confessed breathlessly. Her fingers tangled in his hair; she liked the feel of it.

"Neither had I," he replied. "I wanted to watch you. I still do. Open your mouth a little."

Her heart throbbed as she obeyed him, still looking up into his darkening eyes. Then his teeth nipped and his tongue stroked, and she felt his hands moving her, shifting her, catching her hips to press them intimately into the hard contours of his own. His mouth grew hungry, and her body turned traitor, burning with sweet new fires as she felt his need, emphasized by what his mouth was doing to her, and she went under like a drowning swimmer. Her eyes closed, the pleasure greater than she had expected. Unable to sustain the piercing gaze of his blazing dark eyes, she gave in without the whisper of a protest. She moaned, a strange, long, aching sound in the hot darkness. Her legs trembled against his, her knees curving into his thighs, her stomach pressing into his, her breasts aching as she tried to get closer.

She felt a shudder go through his large body, and then his hand was cupping her breast through the fabric, possessing it, and she panicked.

With a tiny cry, she drew back, catching his hand with cold fingers, her eyes revealing shocked confusion.

He took a deep, harsh breath. "I'm a grown man," he ground out. "What did you expect when you rubbed yourself against me like that?"

She swallowed a harsh retort and eased herself off his lap, back into her own seat, wrapping her arms tightly around herself. "Sorry," she managed in a shaky tone.

He didn't speak. He felt for cigarettes and lit another one with fingers that weren't quite as steady as before. He sat quietly, smoking for a few seconds before he spoke. He looked darkly sensuous, his hair ruffled by her hands, his eyes still black with frustrated passion.

"Presumably, men do touch you from time to time?" he challenged mockingly.

"Not like that, no," she confessed, shooting him a sheepish glance.

He looked shocked. "No mild petting allowed?" he murmured.

She drew a deep breath. She owed him some kind of explanation, at least. "If you want the truth, I don't know a great deal about petting."

"For God's sake, you were married!"

"Yes," she threw back, her eyes bitter. "To a man who looked upon a marriage license as justification for legalized rape!"

6

~~~~~~~~~~

He stared at her for a long time, his face as hard as a statue's, his eyes narrowed and calculating.

She turned her eyes away, embarrassed at the confession she'd never made to anyone except Jan. "I'm sorry I let it go that far," she said tightly. "I can't bear intimacy with a man. I remember all too well what it leads to."

He blew out a heavy cloud of smoke. "My fault," he contradicted, shifting in the seat to place his arm along the back of the seat while he studied her. "I've been a hell of a lot more interested in mergers than women lately. I didn't realize I was that hungry."

She peeked at him out of the corner of her eyes. "If it's any consolation," she told him dryly, "it's

96

been a very long time since I wanted to kiss anyone that much."

One corner of his sensuous mouth curved. "That works both ways," he murmured.

She smiled, lowering her gaze to her wrinkled skirt. "Now I understand why they line up trying to get close to you." She laughed. "And you're crazy if you think it's just because you're rich."

He reached across and untangled one of her hands from her skirt, linking it with his in a slow, exciting caress. "Can you talk about your marriage?" he asked.

She shook her head. "Hurts too much," she confessed. "I went into it with bright eyes and came out crying. It destroyed every illusion I ever had about the pleasures of the boudoir."

He sighed. "He must have hurt you one hell of a lot."

She shrugged. "I was a virgin. I didn't know anything, except what little I had learned from books and listening to other girls talk. I suppose my ignorance made him mad, and things just got worse."

His fingers tightened. "Most men care enough to be gentle the first time."

She laughed bitterly. "Not Larry," she recalled. "It was my fault. Always my fault." She shifted restlessly. "Can we talk about something else, please?"

"In a minute." He turned her face around so that she had to look at him. "Did you ever enjoy it?"

She searched his eyes and smiled faintly. "No,"

she admitted. "I found it painful at first, and then just . . . terribly unpleasant."

"One more question, and I'll leave it alone. Did you ever feel with him what you just felt with me?" he asked gently.

She raised her eyebrows. "If you think I'm going to answer that, you're crazy," she told him.

"Afraid?" he asked silkily.

Her lower lip pouted at him. "Just sensible. You've got a big enough ego as it is."

"Not ego," he said, shaking his head. "Just confidence. In some things," he clarified, smiling. "I'm having to feel my way with you."

She lifted an eyebrow. "Literally?" she murmured.

He laughed softly. "I usually do have more finesse than I've shown tonight. God, woman, you were burning me alive already. All it took to push me over the edge was the feel of you grinding into me that way."

She actually blushed. Her eyes fell to their entangled fingers. She studied his hand, so much darker than her own, enormous, flat-nailed and strong. "I like your hands," she said softly.

His fingers contracted. "I like yours, too, honey," he said. He leaned back against the seat and smoked his cigarette quietly. It was a good silence, secure and comforting and deliciously intimate. She let her head slide sideways onto his arm, and, without a word, he drew her to his side so that she could pillow her cheek on his chest.

"I don't want to," he said after a minute, "but I suppose we'd better go home."

She opened her eyes and looked out the window across his broad chest. "I like being with you," she said quietly.

His arm contracted gently and she felt his breath against her hair. "I like being with you," he murmured. "Very much."

It was like being a girl all over again, on a first date with a special boy. She nuzzled her cheek against him with a sigh.

He crushed out the cigarette and reached for the ignition. She started to move away, but he wouldn't let her.

"No," he said in a strange, soft tone, his eyes holding hers for an instant. "No, stay where you are. I like the feel of you like this."

He started the car and put it into drive, easing it back to the highway. They went all the way to the beach house with his arm holding her like some sweet, fragile treasure.

He came around to open the door for her when they reached the dark house. He caught her hand in his, holding it firmly as they walked to the porch.

"Looks like they've all gone to bed," he observed with a smile.

She looked up at him. "Do you think Jan and Andy are lovers?" she asked.

He glanced down at her. "I don't know," he said quietly. "For both their sakes, I hope it hasn't gone that far. I don't want them forced into marriage by an unwanted pregnancy."

"How do you know that it wouldn't be wanted?" she asked him.

He looked deep into her eyes, his jaw clenching. "Did you want children?" he asked.

She nodded sadly. "More than anything. He didn't."

"It was just as well, under the circumstances," he remarked, and she nodded.

"Did you?" she asked, feeling comfortable enough with him to ask.

For a moment his own mask slipped and she saw the lonely man inside the shell. He nodded.

"And she didn't?" she probed softly.

He laughed bitterly. "She decided that having a baby would ruin her waistline. It wasn't worth the sacrifice."

"Oh, Cal, I'm sorry," she whispered, hurting for him.

He studied her for a long minute, searching her eyes. His chest rose and fell heavily and his eyes darkened. Catching her arm, he drew her back into the shadows beside the door, and pulled her slowly against the length of his body.

"Tell me if I frighten you," he breathed roughly, and bent his head. His mouth opened as it touched hers, parting the soft, trembling line of her lips, his tongue tasting her in a silence that blazed with new sensation, new emotion. She slid her arms hesitantly around his waist, under his unbuttoned jacket, and savored the warmth of his body beneath the thin silk shirt. She melted into him, loving the feel of his powerful legs, the protective warmth of his arms gathering her even closer. Her tongue touched the long, broad line of his upper lip and traced its inner moistness with a totally new sensuality.

He drew back, his breath coming hard. "Don't do that," he whispered roughly.

She searched his dark eyes with a breathless new abandon. "I like the way you taste," she whispered back. Then she smiled up at him, her eyes full of wonder. "You taste smoky."

Involuntarily his mouth tugged into a smile. "You taste like honey. Sweet and smooth and tempting. Much too tempting for this hour of the night," he added. "Unless you'd like to lie in my arms in bed . . . ?"

She tingled from head to toe and her breath caught in her throat as she imagined the picture they'd make—his dark, hair-roughened body poised above her paleness in the dim room, her arms uplifted, welcoming. . . .

"You're blushing," he murmured.

She dropped her eyes and moved away. What she was feeling was too new. "I think I'd better call it a night, Mr. Van Dyne, before I get myself in too deep."

"I was Cal a minute ago," he murmured as he unlocked the door and opened it for her.

She glanced up at him as she went in. "You make me feel like a threatened species." She laughed.

"And I've barely begun," he murmured wickedly. "Come swimming with me in the morning."

She hesitated. "I'd sort of planned to drop a line off the pier and see what I could catch," she admitted.

Both heavy eyebrows arched. "You like to *fish?*" he burst out.

She laughed self-consciously. "Well, surely you've heard that some women do?"

"It wasn't that," he said. "I love it. But I prefer deep-sea fishing."

Her eyes brightened. "Really?"

"I'll hire a boat," he told her. "We'll go for blue marlin, how about that?"

"You'll go for blue marlin," she protested, "and I'll watch. I'm not nearly strong enough for that kind of battle."

"If you'd rather fish from the pier—"

"No," she protested quickly. "Please, I've never been deep-sea fishing."

He laughed softly. "All right. You'll have to get up early."

"Is four o'clock all right?" she asked eagerly.

He touched her cheek lightly, sending delicious shivers down her spine. "Four o'clock is fine," he said softly.

She smiled, and moved reluctantly away from him toward the staircase.

"Margie?"

She turned with her hand on the banister, searching his dark face.

"Wear your hair long tomorrow," he said gently.

She smiled shyly and nodded. Then she went slowly up the steps, dragging her feet, not wanting to leave him. And he watched her every step of the way until she was out of sight.

She was up at three-thirty, despite the few hours' sleep she'd had. She paced the floor restlessly, wanting the hands on the clock to move so that she could see him again.

The sudden knock on her door made her jump. She ran to open it and found Cal standing there, wearing jeans and a red pullover emphasizing his darkness. A light jacket was hooked over his shoulder.

"Ready to go?" he asked, smiling, his eyes moving over her slender body. She had dressed in jeans, a pale green knit shirt and a green sweater with the sleeves pushed up to her elbows.

"Oh yes," she said. "I didn't know if you'd be awake."

"I couldn't sleep," he confessed, the smile fading. "Not one damned minute."

She looked up at him for a long time. "Neither could I," she said gently, watching him.

His fingers tangled in her loosened hair, bringing her face up so that he could touch her mouth with his. It was like touching a flame to dry grass. She caught her breath at the feel of his lips, and her hands gripped his hair-roughened forearms so tightly that they went white under the pressure.

"Oh, God . . ." he groaned, reaching for her.

His foot caught the door, closing it, and he lifted her, with his mouth still covering her own, and carried her to the bed.

"No," she whispered, pleading, as he laid her down on the spotless coverlet that she'd pulled over the neatly made-up sheets.

"I won't take you," he promised, coming down beside her, his chest easing against hers, his arms supporting his formidable weight. "I only want to love you a little," he breathed at her lips. "To taste you and touch you and feel you all up and down my body." His lips brushed teasingly across hers, taunting. He smiled as he felt her involuntary response.

He laughed softly, dragging his chest lightly, abrasively, across her breasts, feeling their helpless response to the sensual pressure.

"Delicious," he breathed into her open mouth. "Like making love to a virgin, feeling those first sweet trembling responses. . . . Still afraid of me, Margie?"

"More than ever," she confessed breathlessly, her eyes wide and full of the newness of wanting. Her hands touched his cheeks, moved down to his throat, the front of his shirt, feeling the warmth and strength of him through it.

"I'll stop whenever you want me to," he said against her mouth. "Kiss me, wildcat. Trust me enough to kiss me properly this time."

And she did, yielding her mouth up to his, letting him do what he pleased with it while her body throbbed and delighted in the nearness of his own above it. Her legs moved, tangling in his, and she clung to him while the kiss went on and on and on.

"Oh yes," he breathed shakily, looking down into her wild eyes. "This is how it feels to make love. To really make love. You didn't know, did you?"

"No," she whispered, feeling the sweet trembling all down her body. "I didn't. Cal . . . ?"

He took a deep breath and ruffled her hair affectionately. "Something you want to know?" he teased gruffly. "Ask me."

"Only if you promise not to make fun of me," she replied, watching him.

He twisted a long strand of her dark hair around his index finger. "I won't laugh."

"Are most men in a terrible hurry once they have a woman in bed with them?" she asked quietly.

"Some men," he said. His eyes searched hers. "Selfish men, who are only interested in their own pleasure."

Her hands pressed against his hard chest, feeling the hard rise and fall of it. She started to ask the next question on her mind, and hesitated.

"No, I'm not," he replied, reading the question in her eyes. "I get nothing out of it unless I give as much pleasure as I take. Is that what you wanted to know?"

She felt her cheeks go hot, but she didn't drop her eyes. "Can it really be good?"

His face hardened, and he touched her cheek lightly. "Poor little scrap," he muttered. "My God, he must have put you through hell to leave such deep scars."

She dropped her eyes to his throat. "Maybe I could have tried harder," she said, sparing herself nothing. "If I had . . ."

"I doubt very much if it would have mattered. Stop looking back. You've done enough of that already." He tugged her hair, forcing her to look up at him. "Well, lovely lady, do we start undressing each other, or do we get up? You may have noticed that you're beginning to have an unmistakable effect on me."

She burst out laughing, exploding inside with the most beautiful sensations. She felt warm and protected and utterly feminine.

He smiled back, dropping a hard kiss on her parted lips before he rolled away from her and got up. He reached down to pull her up beside him.

"Think it's funny, do you?" he growled in mock anger, linking his hands behind her waist to jerk her against him. "Leading a poor defenseless man into your bedroom, wrestling him down on a bed and then tossing him over at the worst time . . . ?"

"Poor defenseless man, my foot." She grinned, linking her hands around his neck. The smile faded as she looked up into his dark, gleaming eyes. "It's magic with you," she said involuntarily, letting the words express her emotions.

He studied her rapt face for a long time before he spoke. "I won't rush you," he promised.

"I know that." She reached up and kissed the line of his jaw gently. "Friends?"

"Unless you've gone numb," he murmured with a wicked smile, "you'll realize that what I'm feeling is a far cry from friendship."

She lifted her chin. "I'm unshockable," she told him, but she drew away from him all the same, and he laughed like a devil.

He picked up his jacket from the floor, where it had fallen minutes before, and gently pushed her out into the hall.

*   *   *

It was the most exciting day she could ever remember. Cal had hired a fishing boat, and she stood beside him while he fought to bring in a fierce blue marlin. The captain and his crew watched with excited faces while the big, dark man in the moving platform chair braced himself and fought for minutes on end while the beautiful marlin leapt and tried to jerk the line away.

Cal laughed the whole time, his eyes on fire with the challenge, his dark face flushed with the pleasure of the battle, and Margie knew she was getting a glimpse of the corporate giant who probably enjoyed battles with his board of directors just as much.

When he finally hauled the huge fish up to the side of the fishing boat, his legs were trembling with the effort of standing.

Margie had jumped and screamed like a fan at a ballgame the whole time, but when she saw the huge, gallant fish hanging out of the water, she felt a surge of pity for it. It had fought so hard only to lose, and it seemed a shame to kill it just for a trophy.

"Don't look so disheartened, honey." Cal chuckled, pulling her close against his side as he turned to tell the skipper to free the huge fish.

Margie could hardly believe her ears. She looked up at him in a daze as the fish was set free, and saw something in his face that she'd missed before.

"He gave it a good shot, didn't he?" The elderly captain grinned at Cal and Margie as they watched the marlin get his bearings and set off quickly away from the fishing boat.

"A run for my money," Cal agreed. "But he looks a hell of a lot better out there than he would on my wall."

The captain nodded, turning back to his duties. "That he does," he agreed with a chuckle. "It's the sport, after all, not the trophy that makes the challenge."

"You're a nice man, Cannon Van Dyne," Margie said quietly, and meant it.

He shrugged. "We don't have such an abundance of wildlife that we can afford to pursue it relentlessly for sport. I don't need trophies to make me feel like a man."

She stood on tiptoe and brushed a kiss across his mouth.

"What was that for?" he asked quietly.

She dropped her eyes, moving closer as the skipper turned the fishing boat back toward the harbor. It had suddenly occurred to her that she'd never known a man who was as much a man as the one standing beside her.

"Hey," he murmured softly, tucking a finger under her chin and raising her face up to his.

She smiled shyly. "What?"

He searched her eyes for a long time. "I've never been with a woman who made me feel the way you do."

"How do I make you feel?" she asked softly.

He touched her mouth lightly with his finger and drew in a long, slow breath. "As if I could conquer the world. You make me feel whole."

He made her feel the same way, but she was still too unsure of herself to admit it. She dropped her eyes and nuzzled her face into his shoulder, hiding it in the soft folds of his jacket.

"Oh, God, don't do that when we're surrounded by people," he groaned, tightening his arm.

"Do what?" she managed.

"Touch me like that," he whispered, catching the hand that had unconsciously found its way into the opening of his shirt and was discovering the warmth of hair-roughened skin just below his collarbone.

"Oh," she breathed, stunned. She hadn't realized what she was doing.

He looked down into her wide eyes. He was breathing heavily, roughly. "We'll go swimming when we get home," he said tautly. "And I'll let you touch me any way you want to."

She hid her face against him, embarrassed, excited, trembling with a kind of pleasure that she'd never experienced before.

"Don't be afraid of it," he whispered, drawing her closer as the boat made its way to shore. "Just let it happen, Margie."

As if she could stop it, she thought dizzily, closing her eyes. She felt as if she were caught in an avalanche, with no way of saving herself. And she wasn't sure that she wanted to.

Jan and Andy were talking to Victorine when they got back to the beach house. Margie found she hated the very thought of other people. She wanted to be alone with Cannon.

Cannon let her hand go with a noticeable reluctance, his eyes holding hers as they walked into the living room.

"Well, where have you two been?" Victorine asked, her eyes amused.

"Deep-sea fishing," Cannon offered, lighting a cigarette.

"Catch anything?" Andy asked.

Cannon laughed. "A blue marlin, but I threw it back. It was just a baby."

"Several hundred pounds worth," Margie murmured with a grin.

"I'll never understand you." Victorine sighed. "Why catch them if you don't intend to keep them?"

"The challenge, Mother," Andy answered for his brother. "It's like mountain climbing, or automobile racing . . . high adventure."

"A trout is pretty exciting, too," Jan murmured, glancing shyly at Cannon. "Margie and Dad and I used to go up into the mountains every year during trout season and wade out into the shallows of the Chattahoochee hoping for a strike."

Cannon actually looked impressed. "Catch many?" he asked the younger girl.

Jan smiled. "My share," she admitted. "But I'm afraid I didn't throw them back. I love broiled trout."

Cannon laughed. "So do I. But marlin doesn't suit my palate."

"Where are you off to now?" Victorine asked Cannon.

He was still watching Margie. "We thought we'd go for a swim," he said absently.

"What a great idea," Andy chimed in, catching Jan around the waist. "We'll join you. Come on, hon, I'll drop you off at your door while you change. Coming, Margie?"

She glanced at Cannon, hoping the disappointment she felt wouldn't show. To her delight, he looked as unhappy about it as she did.

Margie almost turned around and ran when she and Jan got down to the beach. Cannon was waiting for her. He was sensual with all his clothes on, but in a pair of white trunks, he was devastating enough to make her breath catch in her throat.

She was so engrossed in looking at him that she didn't even see Andy come up behind them and lead Jan off into the water. Her eyes were riveted to Cannon. He was bronzed all over, like a painted Greek statue. His chest was matted with curling black hair that arrowed down into his trunks, and his powerful legs were equally sprinkled with black hair. He was the most deliciously masculine man she'd ever seen in a bathing suit, and her hands tingled at the mere thought of touching him.

Sensing that intense scrutiny, he turned his head and looked at her, a cigarette held absently between his fingers. All the mockery, all the antagonism was gone. There was something new in his dark eyes, and Margie felt her knees go weak as she felt the impact of his gaze.

He moved toward her, his eyes going boldly over

her low-cut black and white maillot. His gaze returned pointedly to the small curves of her breasts, revealed by the low v-neck of the top.

He threw away the cigarette and his hands moved to her waist, measuring it as he looked down at her.

"I want to be alone with you," he said quietly.

She managed a teasing smile. "Do you suppose they'd go away if we offered them a quarter apiece?"

He chuckled softly. "Shall we try?"

Her eyes softened as they met his and she felt her body go warm all over at his proximity. "It's happening so fast. . . ." she whispered absently.

"I know." He bent suddenly, lifting her and turning toward the surf. "I hope you can swim," he murmured.

"Like a fish, Mr. Van Dyne." She laughed, clinging to his neck, loving the feel of his hard body against her breasts.

He looked down at her, cocking one eyebrow. "In the nude?" he asked.

She felt the warmth rise in her cheeks. "Actually," she confessed, "I've never done that."

He searched her eyes for a long time. "Would you like to?" he asked deeply. "With me?"

She could hardly breathe. She couldn't break the hold his eyes had on hers, and she was only aware of being in the water when it came up over her breasts, chilling her all at once.

She clung to him, and he laughed at her efforts to stay above water.

"I won't let you drown," he chided. "Just relax. It's not even all that cold."

"It is so," she argued, laughing back at him.

"Oh, I'll keep you warm, if that's your only complaint," he murmured, letting her slide out of his arms. He drew her against him, wrapping her tightly against his body as his legs tangled with hers.

"We'll sink," she whispered, feeling his breath on her lips.

"What a lovely idea," he murmured, glancing over at Jan and Andy, who were playing in the water. "They can't see us kiss if we do it under water, can they?" he asked.

Her lips parted, and she throbbed all over, wanting it.

"Oh, God, come here," he groaned, catching her hair to bring her face toward his. "Hold your breath, darling . . ." he whispered just as his mouth took hers.

They went under together, her mouth locked on his, his hands on her buttocks, pressing her hips against him until she cried out in a soundless moan. Her fingers found the rough hair on his chest, and she clung to him, loving the feel of his body under her palms. She was drowning, out of air, and it didn't matter, because she wanted him enough to die of it.

They broke the surface together, gasping for air, breathless from lack of oxygen and desire. He took her hand firmly and led her back to shore.

"Making love under water has its hazards," he explained with a rueful grin, stretching himself out on the sand and pulling her down beside him. "I didn't want to drown the two of us in the process."

"It was . . . incredible," she whispered, trying to put what she'd felt into words.

"Yes." His eyes traced the lines of her body possessively. "I want you so much I ache, and I can't even touch you."

He caught her hand and drew it to his chest, pressing it palm down into the thick growth of hair, his breath quickening again when her fingers moved on his body. "I want to lie down with you in the sand," he whispered, holding her eyes, "I want to peel that bathing suit off you and put my lips to your skin and taste you. I want to stroke you and tease you until you burn all over with a thousand fires. And then," he whispered, leaning close to her, his voice low as he watched the hunger he'd kindled shimmer in her eyes, "then, I want to ease my body completely over yours and feel you wanting me as much as I want you. . . ."

"Don't," she pleaded in a soft whisper.

"Want me?" he whispered, tracing patterns on her cheek with a slow, maddening finger.

She licked her dry lips. "Yes," she admitted, feeling a shock run through her taut body at the sound of the word.

"And I want you," he whispered. "I'm burning up with it, and as much as I love my brother, right now I damned well wish he were in Singapore and your sister with him!"

She managed a shaky laugh, her face fiery with the fever he'd kindled in her body, her eyes blazing with it. "It's . . . a public beach," she reminded him.

He searched her eyes. "More's the pity." His gaze dropped to his chest, where her fingers were gently exploring his corded muscles.

"You wanted to do this on the boat, didn't you?" he asked quietly.

"Yes," she admitted, watching his chest rise and fall heavily under the gentle pressure of her fingers. She loved the feel of him, the male scent of him.

He glanced back down the beach to find that Jan and Andy had gone out beyond the surf and were swimming away from the beach together.

"Finally," he groaned. "A minute's grace."

He rolled over toward her, his hand on her stomach as he bent and took her mouth under his in a smooth, easy motion.

She pushed at his shoulders, but he lifted his head and shook it gently. "They aren't looking right now," he whispered. "Let's enjoy it while it lasts."

As he spoke his hand moved up between her breasts. While he watched her, his fingers eased under the elastic fabric in a slow, sensuous exploration that caused her to catch her breath and arch helplessly, wanting him to touch her with more than that light, tormenting pressure.

His mouth was poised over hers. "Do you want it?" he breathed softly.

"Please," she whispered, her fingers hovering nervously over his, barely touching.

"Help me, then," he breathed into her mouth as he took it again.

Her fingers guided his, her shoulder moving to
ease the pull of the fabric. She felt his hand engulf
her, skin touching skin, his palm against the hard,
taut rise, and she cried out, the sound taken and
swallowed by his mouth as it became suddenly
possessive, devouring hers in a wave of pleasure
that made her tremble from head to toe.

A minute later, he drew back, his eyes almost
black with frustration, and looked over his shoulder. Andy and Jan were just turning back toward
the shore, and Cannon said something that sounded like a fervent curse.

He looked down at Margie, at his hand touching
her white flesh where he'd pulled the bathing suit to
one side. His hand was dark against her paleness,
and he lifted it just slightly, stroking her, his eyes
apparently fascinated by the helpless reaction of
her body to his touch.

"They'll see," she protested unsteadily.

"I won't let them," he said softly. His eyes
moved back up to hers. "I take back every word I
said about you that first night. The last thing in the
world you need is a padded bra. You're perfect."

She flushed at the adoration in his eyes, at the
feel of his fingers stroking her so intimately.

"Look," he whispered, coaxing her eyes down
to her own body, to the darkness of his fingers
against her skin.

She trembled in reaction, her hand catching his,
her eyes gently pleading with him.

"Embarrassed?" he asked gently. "Here." He
drew the bathing suit back in place with quiet
reluctance, smoothing the shoulder strap down.

She couldn't meet his eyes. She felt like a schoolgirl caught necking with the class hero, and her face burned as she sat up, hugging her knees to her breasts.

He sat up beside her, reaching for the package of cigarettes and lighter beside the bundle of towels on the sand. He lit one with steady fingers as Jan and Andy came running up beside them.

"Gosh, that was fun." Jan laughed, reaching for a towel to dry her hair.

"I could do with a sandwich now," Andy said as he dried his torso with a towel. "Anyone else feeling hungry?"

"I am," Cannon said with a dry laugh, but only Margie knew what he meant. "Let's see if we can raid the refrigerator before Nina starts on supper."

"But you two haven't gone in yet," Jan pointed out.

"We had better things to do," Cannon said as he helped Margie up.

"Now they're suspicious," Margie murmured as they followed the younger couple down the beach.

"Isn't it a good thing they weren't wearing binoculars a minute ago?" he murmured, grinning at the expression on her face.

"I wasn't afraid," she murmured after a moment. "A little embarrassed, yes; it's never been like that for me. But I wasn't afraid."

He stopped, turning her toward him, and linked his hands around her waist. His dark eyes searched hers for a long time. "You're not frigid," he said softly. "And I can get rid of every one of those scars, if you'll let me."

"I know," she admitted. Her eyes dropped to his wide, chiseled mouth. "It's just that it's happening so quickly. . . ."

He touched his finger to her mouth, silencing the words. "I'll give you time to get used to me first," he said. "I won't take more than you want to give."

But she wanted to give him everything, and she was only just realizing it. She turned and fell into step beside him without replying. But her hand, in his, tightened.

Margie had wondered how she was going to keep her eyes away from Cannon that evening—so that the family wouldn't see her helpless interest in him. But fate solved the problem for her. Cannon was invited to a banquet that night—one he'd apparently forgotten until some woman with a sexy voice called to remind him.

Margie had answered the phone, being the closest one to it, and her eyes followed Cannon while he spoke to the caller. His expression hadn't been one of pleasure, but his deep lazy voice had a different pitch to it, a note that spoke of long acquaintance. As soon as he'd hung up he excused himself to go dress.

Jan and Andy had decided to take in a movie and were already gone when he came back down. Victorine was engrossed in her favorite television show, and Margie, lacking anything more pressing, was watching it with her, despite the fact that her book deadline was looming closer by the day.

"I'll be getting home late, I'm afraid," Cannon

told his mother as he bent to kiss her cheek. "Don't wait up."

"I wouldn't dare," the elderly woman teased. "Who is she, or am I allowed to ask?"

"Missy Caller," he said, "and her brother. It's about that damned Seaside contract we've been trying to get—an exclusive on their swimwear fashions."

"Surely you can wink at Missy and get anything you want." His mother laughed.

He didn't smile, and his eyes were troubled as they studied Margie's averted face. "Margie, come outside with me," he said curtly.

She glanced at him, uncertain, ignoring Victorine's pointed stare. "I . . ."

He held out his hand. Just that, but it was enough. She got up, mumbled something to Victorine, and let him take her by the hand and lead her out into the sea-scented night air.

"I don't want to go," he said quietly, turning to face her when he reached the car. "If this contract weren't important, I'd forget the whole damned thing. Despite what Mother said, I have no personal interest in Missy. Only a business one."

She looked up at him. "I don't have any claim on you," she reminded him.

"I know. Maybe I want you to have one," he said surprisingly. He touched her cheek lightly. "We'll find something different to do tomorrow— someplace where Andy and Jan can't find us."

"It might be better if we didn't," she said softly, remembering how vulnerable she'd become with him.

His dark gaze lanced down at her. He caught her face in his warm hands and held it up to his. "You don't have a single reason to be afraid of me," he said shortly.

"It isn't that," she protested weakly. His touch was devastating.

His thumbs edged toward her full mouth and brushed over it sensuously. "Is your Victorian upbringing raising its ugly head?" he murmured dryly.

She couldn't help laughing. "I know. It's the twentieth century, isn't it?"

He bent and gently pressed his mouth against hers, a kiss that was soft and tender and poignant. "Suppose we let each day take care of itself?" he suggested in a deep, lazy tone. "Besides," he added, "you're the one who wrestles me down on beds and forces me to do intimate things to you. . . ."

"You wicked man!" she breathed in her best stage whisper.

"Dirty young woman," he countered, bending his head again. His open mouth brushed against hers. "Damn Missy," he murmured.

Margie's green eyes peered up at him. "Is she pretty?"

He cocked an eyebrow, studying her shimmering eyes, her long, waving dark hair, her complexion, soft and creamy in the muted light. "Compared to you, no woman is."

"You're not bad, either." She laughed.

He drew in a deep breath. "I'd ask you to wait

up, but I don't have any idea when I'll get home. Suppose we meet at the breakfast table at six?"

Her eyebrows lifted. "Shall I wear a trenchcoat?"

His eyes gleamed. "How about a see-through negligee?"

Her fist connected with his chest. "Stop that."

He grinned. "Why don't you put on a dress and come with me?"

She shook her head. "I don't want to spend my evening watching other women drool over you."

The smile faded slowly, and his eyes were shrewd as they searched hers, seeing through the teasing to the truth.

He caught her by the waist and lifted her up to him so that her lips were level with his. "Kiss me good night and go back in. It's chilly out here, and you don't have a wrap."

That one expression of concern made her want to cry. Only Jan had ever cared what happened to her. It was new to be worried about. She stemmed the tears by pressing her lips to his, her arms going around to hold him while he kissed her back, slowly, sweetly, endlessly.

He lifted his head after a minute, his eyes dark and strangely soft. "Good night," he murmured.

"Good night," she whispered.

But he was already kissing her again, and this time it was neither soft nor brief. When he let her slide back to the ground, she felt as if she were on fire all the way to her toes.

"I'm going," he said curtly, "while I still can. 'Night."

She stood and watched him until he drove out of the gates.

Victorine gave Margie a brief, amused glance when she sat back down on the sofa to watch television.

"He really isn't attached to Missy," she offered gently.

Margie smiled. "I think I'd rip her eyes out if he were," she admitted with a sheepish grin.

The older woman laughed gently and reached out to pat her hand. "I'm very glad that you and I get along so well," she murmured. "You'll be able to help me find new ways to get around Cannon."

It was too soon to be thinking that way, but Margie wanted the fiction so badly that she didn't even offer a protest.

The program was almost over when the phone rang, and Margie picked it up, surprised to find her agent on the other end of the line.

"Why aren't you at home?" he grumbled. "I've looked high and low, and I finally got your answering service; the lines had been out. . . . Anyway—"—his tone brightened—"I've got great news. Remember Gene Murdock? Well, he wants to talk about a movie contract on your last book, and he's only going to be in town until late tomorrow. He wants to have you in on the discussion. Can you be in my office by ten in the morning?"

7

~~~~~~~~~~~~~~~~~~

She couldn't even answer him. Since she'd arrived in Panama City, the book had been the furthest thing from her mind. It seemed in some strange way to belong to another life, not the one she was involved in with Cannon Van Dyne.

"Uh, in the morning?" she stammered.

"Feeling okay, love?" He laughed. "Remember who you are? Silver McPherson, author of *Blazing Passion,* that number one bestseller for the past four weeks . . . ?"

"Sure, I remember," she agreed numbly. "Ten o'clock in the morning. Well, if I can get a flight out at seven . . . I'll do my best. If I can't make it, I'll call you, okay?"

"Okay. And congratulations! This one looks like a winner. See you!"

She stared at the receiver in her hand, aware of Victorine's brief, puzzled gaze. New York in the morning. She'd almost surely have to stay overnight, and just the thought of being away from Cannon that long was torture. What was the matter with her? Once, a movie contract would have been the biggest thing in the world to her, but now it was only a barrier between herself and Cannon—another brick in the wall her deception was building between them. Someday he was going to find out about her notorious profession, and what would he think? He'd be furious that she hadn't told him the truth, that was certain. And how would her nom de plume affect his very conservative image? She felt a wave of pain so sweeping it brought a mist of tears to her eyes.

"Are you all right, my dear?" Victorine asked gently.

Margie started, glancing at her. "Oh, yes," she said numbly. "It, uh, it was just some business I have to see about tomorrow. Something to do with dividends. . . ." she concluded vaguely, leaving Victorine to draw her own conclusions.

"Thank goodness I have Cannon to keep up with my finances," the older woman replied. "And there's no need to worry about a commercial flight. Cannon will fly you up."

"I couldn't ask him . . ." Margie began nervously.

"Of course you can. Now come and watch television with me and don't worry, dear. Everything will work itself out," she promised.

Margie sat back down, but her eyes were troubled. What would she do if Cannon decided to go with her? How would she keep him from finding out why she was going?

She hardly slept at all, brooding over it. She and Cannon had become so close—so quickly—that she hadn't had time to come to grips with the problems. Now they were staring her in the face. She no longer had any logical reason for keeping the truth from him. Not one that he'd accept, anyway.

It didn't help when Jan came bouncing into her room beaming as she perched herself on the edge of Margie's bed.

"Cannon's flying you to New York this morning," she burst out. "What is it, something to do with the book?"

Margie turned over, her eyes smarting from the early morning sun, her head hurting. "Yes," she mumbled. "A movie contract."

"A movie!" Jan burst out. "What kind?"

"For television," she managed, dragging herself up. "What time is it?"

"Six, and what do you mean, glowering like that?" Her sister laughed. "You're going to be famous!"

"I don't want to be famous," she grumbled. "I wish I'd never written the first book. I wish I were in China!"

Jan stared at her. "Huh?"

"Never mind." She lowered her face to her drawn-up knees. "How in the world am I going to explain to Cannon why I'm going to New York?" she moaned.

Jan sobered at once. "Now I understand. He's gotten to you, hasn't he?"

Margie laughed weakly. "That's one way of putting it."

Jan moved closer and put a comforting arm around her. "Oh, Margie, and I'm the idiot who begged you not to tell him about Silver Mc-Pherson."

"It's okay," Margie said softly. "It will all work out somehow."

Jan drew back, her eyes speculative. "Are you in love with him?"

The question, put into words, was devastating. Margie felt herself color, her eyes glowing with the answer.

Jan only nodded. "It was so obvious yesterday. He could hardly take his eyes off you, and you were looking at him as though he were the best part of the menu. . . ."

"He wants me," Margie corrected, studying her drawn-up knees. "And as we both know, I have quite a problem in that respect."

"No, you haven't," Jan argued gently. "Not if you love him. It will all come naturally, you'll see."

"It means a kind of commitment that terrifies me, though. Don't you see?" Margie ground out. "I'm not the type for one-night stands; I'm not built for them. I can't give myself just to satisfy a craving!"

"You little old Victorian, you," Jan teased softly. "Believe me, if you love him the way I think you do, you won't be able to say no. Sad, but true."

Margie lifted her eyes, and everything she felt was in them. "He snuck up on me." She laughed. "Oh Jan, I love him until it hurts!"

"I'm very glad," her sister said. "I was afraid you were going to make do with writing all your life. It would have been such a terrible waste, Margie."

"But how am I going to explain to him what I do for a living?" Margie sighed. "It's such a mess!"

"And you're a worry-wart." Jan got up. "Come on, you'd better get a move on. Margie . . . can I ask you just one big favor—the last one, I swear?"

"You know you can."

Jan shrugged. "Would you kind of mention to Cannon that, well, that Andy and I would even be willing to wait a few months—to be away from each other that long—to show him that we're sure of each other?" She smiled. "And maybe butter him up just a little . . . ?"

"You wicked child," Margie accused. She threw back the covers and stood up, stretching. "But, yes, I will talk to him, if he'll listen."

"Ask him when you're dressed like that," Jan suggested, indicating the see-through gown. "He'll listen." She grinned, and had barely gotten out of the room before the pillow was flung at her.

Cannon was at the breakfast table with the rest of the family when Margie came in with her suitcase and purse in hand. She put them down inside the doorway, tingling as she felt his eyes take in the immaculate white linen suit she was wearing with a beige blouse and beige accessories.

"I hear we're going to New York," he murmured

with a faintly wicked smile that was meant for her alone.

"I . . . I could always get a commercial flight," she stammered, sitting down quickly in the chair he drew out for her.

"Don't be ridiculous," he said. "We'll take in the sights while we're there."

She glanced at him shyly, reading all kinds of secrets in his dark eyes. "If you're sure you don't mind?"

He laughed. "Not at all. We'll stay the night and fly back tomorrow."

"Cannon has a suite at one of the hotels there," Victorine volunteered. "He spends a lot of time in New York on business, you know. It's quite comfortable, and the food in the dining room is delicious!"

"And there's a lock on the bedroom door," Cannon murmured, watching her hunted expression and laughing wickedly when the others started chuckling.

"Don't you dare seduce her," Victorine informed her eldest, her face haughty. "I refuse to have my friend become just another of your conquests."

Cannon grinned at his mother, looking devilishly handsome in a tailored grey vested suit that made him look darker and larger than ever. "She'd never be that," he said, and his expression changed, softening, intensifying, when he looked at Margie.

Victorine saw the look and dropped her eyes, smiling into her coffee.

* * *

Margie sat quietly beside Cannon in the cockpit, watching his deft hands work the controls as the small jet darted up into the clouds.

She'd thought after Larry's death that she could never bear to fly in a small plane again, but flying with Cannon was an experience. He was careful and confident, and she felt safer with him than she'd ever felt with another human being. It was odd how comfortable they were together, despite the fact that her pulse rate never seemed to slow down around him. She watched him handle the plane and wondered if he'd handle her as gently, as confidently. She was almost sure that he would, and she was more afraid than ever of what lay ahead.

Cannon's hotel suite was deliciously luxurious, but Margie barely had time to put down her suitcase before she had to rush out and catch a cab to her agent's office. She left Cannon in the suite with a convincing story about having to discuss some legality with her husband's attorney. She hated the lie even as she was telling it, and she decided then that she was going to have to find a way to tell him the truth.

Her agent, Jim Payne, was waiting in his office for her, all smiles as he guided her to a seat beside Gene Murdock, who was half her agent's size and twice his age and full of enthusiasm for the project of converting her bestselling saga of the Revolutionary War to film.

The discussion took a long time, but by the end of it she was convinced that Murdock would do a good packaging job. More important, Jim was convinced of it. They agreed on a contract, which would provide her with an advance that would make her future relatively secure. She shook hands with both men and got into the elevator in a daze.

One thing was certain, she realized: she was going to have to tell Cannon the truth quickly. The publicity would be out any day, and Silver McPherson would become even more notorious than she already was. She couldn't bear it if Cannon found out from a third party. It would make her look even more guilty.

She went back to the hotel to find him on the phone, his dark brows drawn together, his lips making a thin line as he listened to whoever was on the other end of the receiver.

"No," he said curtly, glancing toward Margie as she came in the door. "No, that's not going to work. I told you, my attorney advised me to have that clause changed, and I'm not signing a damned thing until it's done. Can I what? Oh, hell," he growled, sighing roughly. "All right, where? What time? I'll be there." He hung up the phone with a bang.

"Trouble?" she asked.

He studied her, his hands jammed into his pockets. "Nothing I can't handle. Unfortunately, it looks as if it's going to take the rest of the day. I had a lot planned for us to do together."

She shrugged. "I understand about business," she said, smiling. "It's all right."

"It most damned well is not," he ground out, moving toward her. He took her by the shoulders and pulled her slowly, sensuously, against his powerful body, his breathing suddenly as unsteady as her own. "Now, is it?" he challenged, and his hands caught her hips, urging them against his taut thighs in a lazy, disturbing motion.

She caught his hands, but that didn't even slow him down.

"That's it," he murmured, his parted lips descending to her mouth. "Help me. . . ."

She caught her breath as he moved, and she felt the hunger in him even before his mouth coaxed hers to open for the hot, hungry penetration of his tongue.

She moved, too, rocking with him as the magic of being in his arms worked on her, melted her. Her fingers went to the buttons of his shirt and tremulously opened the top four.

"Do you want to touch me?" he breathed into her mouth.

"Terribly," she admitted in a stranger's husky voice. Her fingers eased the fabric aside so that they could tangle in the thick hair on his warm chest.

He drew back a little, his breath catching as he watched her hands on his bare chest. "Lie down with me," he said gruffly. "Let's do it properly."

She looked up and took a deep, steadying breath. "You've got a meeting."

"I could miss it," he said shortly.

"But you shouldn't," she murmured, reading his eyes.

He sighed heavily. "No," he admitted.

She bent forward and touched her lips gently to

his chest before she started buttoning buttons again, feeling him shudder at the light caress.

"I'd better buy a deadbolt for your bedroom door while I'm out," he suggested gruffly. "And you'd better pile furniture against it."

"I'll dig a Burmese tiger trap at the doorway while you're gone," she promised, but her eyes were adoring.

He bent and kissed her, very gently. "I'll be back as soon as I possibly can," he promised. "Will you miss me?"

"I already do," she said, and it was no lie.

He smiled, touching her cheek before he turned and went out the door.

They had supper at the hotel restaurant, and Margie found that she had a great appetite, fostered by the incredible happiness she felt by simply being with Cannon.

He was unusually attentive. His eyes never left her, straying constantly to the low neckline of her silver gown where it clung lovingly to every soft curve. He was a dish himself in evening clothes, so handsome that other women openly stared.

"If that redhead doesn't stop ogling you," she murmured over her dessert, "I'm going to take this delicious wine and pour a glass of it over her head."

He laughed softly. "What a waste of good wine," he said. He lifted the bottle and poured her another glass. It was an aged burgundy, very smooth, and she'd had more than enough already, but she was ignoring her own conscience. It might be the last evening she'd ever spend with him, because tonight she was going to tell him the truth about herself—if it killed her.

"Are you trying to get me drunk?" she murmured demurely.

"Not at all," he replied, watching her over the rim of his own glass. "Just . . . relaxed."

"You aren't really drunk, are you?" he asked when they were back in the suite. Watching her closely, he shed his jacket and tie and flicked open the buttons of his shirt.

"I'm only relaxed," she promised him. Feeling provocative and bubbling with happiness, she went to him and put her arms around his neck. "Very, very relaxed." Her eyes clouded. The smile faded as she met his searching gaze. "And very, very much in love," she whispered, the words slipping out so smoothly that she hardly realized she'd spoken aloud.

"Oh, God, honey," he murmured, bending. His mouth took hers in a new, sweet way. She moved closer, hungry for him, loving him, needing him . . . wanting him!

His hands found the tiny straps that held her dress in place and eased them aside so that his mouth could brush softly across the soft, scented flesh of her shoulders, her neck, her throat—and lower, to the high, rounded curves of her breasts. He made an impatient sound deep in his throat and she felt the coolness of the room on her bare flesh as the dress fell suddenly into a sparkling puddle around her silver high heels.

Her eyes opened and she started to protest, but

his mouth was taking possession of the curves he'd uncovered, his tongue teasing pink peaks into hard, sensitive points. His hands found new softness, touching, probing, faintly abrasive against silken skin, so confident and careful, so expert. . . .

She moaned, arching against him, encouraging him, deaf to the tiny voice at the back of her mind that urged caution and restraint. She was so lost in sensation that she could hardly breathe at all. Her body belonged to him, and it was telling him so in every nerve, every cell.

She felt him lift her up in his hard, sure arms, and put his mouth gently, tenderly to hers.

"I'm too old for careless encounters," he breathed into her mouth, "and so are you. If you let me have you, it's going to mean a commitment. Do you hear me? It won't be just sex."

"I love you," she whispered back. "I love you. . . ."

"I'll never let you go, Margie," he vowed as he carried her down the long, dark hall. "Not as long as I live."

"Don't hurt me," she whispered, a last tiny surge of fear trembling through her.

"Sweet treasure," he murmured huskily, "that's the one thing I'm not going to do. . . ."

She clung tightly, her mouth lovingly tracing the hard lines of his face as he carried her into his own bedroom and closed the door behind them. The bed was soft under her back, and his formidable weight rocked her gently as he settled onto it beside her.

"The light, Cannon," she whispered.

"Don't you want to watch?" he murmured just above her mouth. "I do."

Her heart pounded furiously. She lay still against the pillows, watching him as he sat up and gazed long and intently at the length of her silken body, clad only in her panties. She knew she was blushing, but she couldn't help it. Larry, the only other man who'd seen her like this, had never cared for the sight of her "skinny body."

"If I weren't such a jealous man," Cannon said finally, his voice unsteady, "I'd have you painted like this. But I couldn't bear to have an artist see you this way. No other man. Only me." He bent and touched her mouth tenderly with his own. His fingers traced a sweet, abrasive path around one perfect breast with an expertise that was shattering.

"Are you mine, Margie?" he asked.

"Yes," she said without hesitation. She reached up to draw him down against her. "Always. As long as I live . . . longer. . . ."

He slid his hands under her bare back, lifting, his palms warm against her silken flesh as he brought her up to him and kissed her softly. He eased his weight down on her yielding body so that she could feel every hard contour of him, the fabric of his clothing rough against her bareness. She moaned gently.

"You see how good it can be?" he whispered. His lips brushed hers, his teeth ardently catching and pulling the lower lip. "Here, darling," he murmured, drawing her hand to the buttons of his shirt. "Open it."

With a deftness she was unaware of, her fingers

coaxed the buttons open and slid the silky fabric away from his broad, tanned shoulders, feeling the warmth and power in them with awe. She liked the way his skin felt under her fingers, the hardness of muscle, the sensuous maleness of the thick carpet of hair that made a wedge across his broad chest. She stroked it, tugging gently at the tangle of it, and smiled when she elicited a harsh groan from the mouth that was ardently crushing her own.

"You little witch," he ground out, raising himself up to look at her smiling face, at the green eyes shimmering with raw excitement. "That was deliberate."

"Accidental," she murmured. Her hands slid onto his shoulders, his neck. "Larry never liked me to touch him," she recalled, and her smile faded with the memory. "He didn't like to touch me either, or look at me. . . ."

"Stop looking back," he said softly, holding her gaze while his fingers moved expertly down her body and made it go taut with desire. "You're with me now, and I want to touch every inch of you."

"I may disappoint you. . . ."

"Never," he said quietly. "You make me feel whole. You're everything I've ever wanted in a woman, all the secret dreams a man hoards of his ideal. In no way could you ever be a disappointment."

Tears blurred his image. She reached up to touch the long, masculine curve of his mouth. "Oh, I love you so!"

He moved, so that their bodies were touching at every point, her soft breasts crushed against the mat of hair on his chest, her legs brushing his, mingling with them as they strained together.

"It's going to happen," he whispered shakily as they kissed more intimately, the hunger they felt for each other overpowering. "I can't stop."

"I don't want you to stop," she moaned, arching. "Love me. Love me, make it stop aching!"

"Oh, God, what a sweet ache," he breathed. His mouth was careful with hers, so tender that she could have cried. His hands gentled her, tracing slow patterns, preparing her for him.

"I've never wanted . . . anyone before," she confessed as he pressed her back into the pillows. "I never loved . . . until now."

"Be quiet, darling," he whispered. "Lie still, and do what I tell you. . . ."

"How wicked," she said, trembling, waiting to be overwhelmed, possessed, taken. . . .

"Not half as wicked as what I'm going to do to you now," he promised with a triumphant smile when his hands moved and she cried out. "Yes," he said breathlessly, watching her. "Oh yes, that's it, darling, welcome me. . . ."

His hand went to his belt a wild minute later, then froze as the sudden sharp buzz of the doorbell burst into the silence like a bomb blast, shattering the silver intimacy into a thousand ragged shards, bringing back ice-cold sanity. And Cannon cursed like a drunken sailor, his face terrible.

"I hope whoever's at that damned door has his life insurance paid up," he said under his breath as he sat up and fought to calm his rapid pulse and ragged breathing.

"Oh, God . . . !" he groaned. His shoulders shuddered as he buried his face in his hands for a minute, his body rigid.

"I never would have stopped you," she whispered. "I'm sorry."

He drew in a harsh breath and eased his shoulders back. He glanced down at her with lingering regret as she pulled up the covers to her chin.

"What a shame," he said softly, "to cover up such beauty."

She managed a strained smile for him. "I've only just realized where I am, and why," she confessed with a mischievous gleam in her eyes. "You heartless seducer . . ."

"Me?" he burst out in mock outrage, standing up to find his shirt and tug it back on. "Like hell. You dragged me in here and tried to seduce me!"

"I never!" she retorted. She sat up, tossing back her dark, disheveled hair. "A gentleman . . ." she began, stressing the word.

"I'm not a gentleman," he reminded her, glaring toward the hall where the doorbell was being repeatedly jabbed. "And you damned sure wouldn't love me if I were, would you?" he added with a grin.

She peeked up at him through her lashes. "I'll let you know when I've had several hours to think about it. You'd better see who it is. Maybe somebody called the police when they saw you bring a sweet young thing like me into your evil lair."

"You're sweet, all right," he murmured, going toward the door. "If you'll stay just as you are until I get rid of our company, I'll express that a little more physically."

"Oh, I've had my excitement for tonight, thanks," she said. "I think . . . I'd like to do a little more thinking."

He looked back at her, but he wasn't angry—or even impatient. He smiled. "We'll go at your pace, honey. I want you, but I'm not going to force you. See you in the morning."

She nodded. " 'Night."

He winked as he went out.

The intruder was a business associate of Cannon's who wanted to discuss the contractual agreement he'd been working on all day. Margie was secretly grateful for the opportunity to steal away to her own bedroom and lock herself in. The wine had banished her inhibitions momentarily, but the interruption had brought them back with fresh intensity. Not only had she been willing to lay aside all her principles, she'd even admitted to him that she loved him!

She put on her gown and climbed into bed, her mind still on the feel of his hands, his warm, powerful body against her own bareness, the sweet aching crush of his mouth. She did love him—that was no lie. She ached for him in ways she couldn't have imagined before.

And while he hadn't admitted to sharing those feelings, he'd admitted to her that she was everything he wanted in a woman.

Of course, she reminded herself brutally, men

were likely to say anything when they wanted a woman, regardless of whether or not it was true. And Cannon very definitely wanted her, she remembered, blushing.

She turned out the light and pulled the covers over her. In the morning, with a clear head, she'd think about it again. But right now, her fuzzy mind was only fit for sleep, not for untangling emotional puzzles.

The following morning she awoke with a start, sitting straight up in the wide bed. She bit her lower lip as she began to remember, her eyes closing when bits and pieces of what had happened came back to her.

Her long legs swung off the bed and she went to her suitcase, dragging out a pair of navy slacks and a white blouse. She hurried into the bathroom and showered quickly, grateful for the blow dryer that restored some order to her hair. She used more makeup than usual to camouflage the shadows under her eyes, the faintly bruised mouth. Reality seemed harsher by the morning's light than it had the night before. She was glad now that the interruption had prevented her from making love to Cannon.

"Idiot!" she berated herself. "Oh, you idiot!"

She didn't know how she was going to face him. If only she hadn't had all that wine. If only she'd pulled away. . . .

She packed her suitcase methodically and gathered it and her purse, slinging her navy blazer around her shoulders. She opened the door and walked slowly down the hall.

Cannon was in the sitting room, uncovering dishes apparently left by room service. There were eggs, sausages, toast and coffee, all laid out on the small table.

He looked up as she came into the room, his hard arms shown to their best advantage in a short-sleeved yellow knit shirt. His eyes were as bloodshot as her own, and the dark shadows under them had no camouflage of makeup as hers did.

"Good morning," she managed in a tight, husky voice, avoiding his dark eyes.

"Good morning," he replied with equal reserve. "Sit down and we'll have a quick breakfast before we head back to Florida."

She sat, placing a napkin in her lap before she picked up her coffee and sipped it.

He seated himself across from her, and neither of them spoke while they ate small amounts of the food. Cannon's dark, troubled eyes watched her the whole time.

"Margie," he said softly.

She looked up, her fork poised over the delicious scrambled eggs that she'd hardly touched. She saw her own regrets mirrored in his hard face.

"Nothing happened," he reminded her.

She smiled wistfully. "By the skin of our teeth," she observed.

"And if it had, would the world have ended?" he asked. He got up, kneeling beside her chair with one arm across her knees, one hand curving around her waist. "Answer me. If I'd had you last night, would it have been so terrible?"

"You said it yourself," she sighed. "I have a very Victorian outlook on life, a legacy from Grandmother McPherson who thought that a girl should fling herself out a window if she let herself be seduced."

"Doesn't it depend on who does the seducing?" he asked dryly.

"Not to her, it didn't." She looked into his dark, smiling eyes and relaxed for the first time that morning. "It was the wine, you know," she told him softly.

"I'm afraid I don't believe that," he replied. He touched her thigh, and her leg tautened involuntarily at the sensuous caress. "We wanted each other, Margie. There's no shame in that. It's the most human thing in the world."

Her lower lip thrust gently forward. "It's cheap."

Both eyebrows went up over laughing eyes. "Not in my income bracket, it isn't." He chuckled.

She hit his shoulder with the palm of her hand. "Stop that," she chided. "You know what I mean. People can . . . make love to each other without strings these days. Except that I can't be casual about it."

He drew in a slow breath, studying her averted face quietly for a long time. "I didn't tell you what I felt, did I?" he asked. His fingers moved up to her chin, turning her eyes back to his. "Did you think it was all physical with me? That you were just going to be another notch on the bedpost?"

"It's nothing against you," she replied matter-of-factly. "You're a man."

"And you're a woman. Very much a woman. The first woman," he added with a level look, "that I've touched in several months. I work hard and I play hard, but I don't have affairs. Not even brief ones."

"Just the occasional one-night stand?"

"That's about the size of it," he admitted. "And even then I'm damned particular about the woman. Since my divorce, I haven't cared all that much for commitment."

She studied his hard face intently.

"Looking for scars? They don't show," he told her.

She shook her head. "I'm trying to imagine what kind of woman would attract you enough to get you to the altar."

His sensuous mouth curved. "She was a voluptuous redhead and I literally lost my head over her. I was twenty-five, fresh out of college with a vice-presidency under my belt and visions of love everlasting in my mind. She cured me in two years, and I divorced her the night I found her latest lover in my bed."

"Did you know him?" she asked.

He laughed. "He was her interior decorator."

"She went from you . . . ?" Her tone was incredulous.

He studied her. "You say that as if you couldn't imagine a woman going from me to another man."

"I can't," she confessed, and turned her face away. "We'd better finish our breakfast."

"What would you say," he said softly, catching her fingers to lock them into his, "if I were to tell you that I couldn't go from you to another woman?"

She felt her eyes dilating, her lips parting as she met his quiet, unblinking gaze. "Are you . . . telling me that?"

He brought her fingers to his mouth and kissed them softly. "Yes, I am." He turned her hand, and touched his mouth to her palm. His breath sounded uneven and his fingers crushed hers. "Margie, if you want the moon, I'll get it for you," he whispered half in jest. "Just promise me you won't ever try to walk away from me."

Tears misted her green eyes as she watched him get to his feet and pull her up against him. His arms swallowed her against his large, powerful body, and he cradled her gently. What could she say? In just a few hours, she was going to be back in Panama City, and she was going to have to tell him the truth. She saw now that there was no future for them as long as any pretense lay between them. She was going to have to trust him enough to level with him, and it might be the end of everything.

"I won't go unless you send me away," she compromised, and pressed close to him, drinking in the scent of him.

"Send you away?" He laughed mirthlessly. "My God, ask me to do something simple, like cutting off an arm; it would be less painful." His arms tightened. "Margie, I . . . want you."

It sounded as if he was saying one thing, but meaning something very different. Her breath caught and she looked up at him. "Cannon, when we get back, I've got something to confess; something that I . . . have to tell you. And you may not like it, or me."

He cocked an eyebrow. "You're not on the pill—is that it?" he murmured wickedly.

She smothered a grin. "Actually, I'm not, but that isn't what I have to tell you."

"Then what is it?"

He looked so concerned, so genuinely concerned, that she almost told him right then. But the words stuck in her throat.

"Not today," she said.

"All right. Not today." He took her by the waist and lifted her up against his body so that her lips were level with his. "I dreamed about you," he murmured as he tugged her closer. "I dreamed . . . that we made love. . . ." His mouth nudged her lips apart, bit at them, teased them. "It was so real that I woke up in a cold sweat and reached for you."

Her arms went around his neck and she nuzzled her nose against his, smiling lazily, lovingly. "Was I there?" she murmured.

He chuckled. "It felt like you," he murmured back, "but when I opened my eyes, I was squeezing the hell out of a feather pillow."

"I didn't realize I was that flabby," she whispered as he kissed her.

"That soft," he corrected. "And only in certain places. Here . . . for instance," he added, lifting her higher so that his mouth could reach the soft swell of her breasts. Even through the fabric the kiss was shatteringly intimate, and she caught her breath with an audible gasp.

He let her slide down his body until her feet reached the floor, and his eyes probed hers for a long time. "All I have to do is look at you," he said in a deep, quiet tone, "and I ache to the soles of my shoes. Sorcery. Witchcraft."

"You cast a few spells of your own, you know," she replied. Her hands flattened on his chest, feeling the powerful muscles contract at the light, sensuous touch. "I wondered when we met if you were as hairy all over as your forearms were. Did you know?" She laughed suddenly, her eyes lighting mischievously as she looked up.

He burst out laughing and linked his hands behind her to swing her with rough affection from side to side. "I am," he murmured, "as you almost found out last night."

"I've decided that I like hairy men," she returned. "It gives me something to do with my hands."

"What does, pulling all the hairs out?" he chided. He jerked her close. "My God, you're tying me in knots. I don't want commitment, but I'll be damned if I could stand a brief affair with you. In between making money and giving it away, you're all I think about."

"I'm very glad," she said. "Because you've been all I've thought about since the first time I saw you."

"Oh, honey," he whispered shakily. He took her mouth with such tender sweetness that tears welled up in her eyes. She held his face between her hands, holding his mouth over hers while the kiss went on and on and on.

After a long minute, he gently pushed her away from him with a heavy sigh. "No more of that for the moment," he said huskily. "For the next few days, we're going to get to know one another in a strictly verbal sense."

She studied him quietly. "And then?"

He smiled slowly. "I think you already know. I do."

Her eyes were troubled. "There's so much you don't know about me."

"I'll learn," he murmured. He kissed her softly. "Let's go."

"Cannon . . ."

He turned at the doorway, with her suitcase in his hand. "What, honey?"

"What about Andy and Jan?" she asked quietly.

He laughed at her worried expression. "You know damned well I'd give you anything you wanted right now. I'll give them my blessing, all right?"

Her face lit up. At least one good thing was going to come out of all this subterfuge, she thought miserably. At least Jan would be happy.

"Thank you," she said, smiling.

He drew her to his side as they went toward the door. "I only hope they'll be as happy as we are," he said softly.

8

~~~~~~~~~~~~~~~~

She was to remember those words later, when they landed in Panama City. And remember them vividly. She followed him into the air terminal, holding the sleeve of his lightweight tan jacket as she tried to keep up with his long strides. It was there that providence overtook her.

"My gosh, it's you!" a wild voice gushed out as a woman with white hair positioned herself directly in front of Margie and looked back and forth from the inside cover of *Blazing Passion* to Margie's face.

Margie quelled the urge to run. It wouldn't do a bit of good.

"Isn't it a marvelous likeness?" the woman asked, handing the book to Cannon. He stared in fascination at the small photo of Margie inside the front cover of the bestselling book. "I'd have known her anywhere! When is your next book coming out, Miss McPherson?" the woman continued, blissfully ignorant of the disaster she'd just precipitated. "I read everything you write!"

"It, uh, it will be out early next year," Margie managed. "Excuse me, please . . ."

She rushed past the woman, who was just getting the book back from a glowering, harsh-faced Cannon. She felt her world coming to an end, and she fought back a flood of hot tears as she waited outside in the blazing heat for him to join her.

It didn't take long. She felt him before she saw him, raising her eyes to his reluctantly.

"Well, well," he said coldly. "A few political articles for the local paper, didn't you say?"

She dropped her eyes to his shirt and drew in a deep, slow breath. "I thought you were a very conventional man," she said quietly. "I was afraid of spoiling Jan's chances with Andy by telling you the truth. I'm . . . I'm fairly notorious."

"Yes," he agreed curtly, "you are that. I've seen the damned book on half the desks in the secretarial pool, and the cover's been screaming at me from bookstore counters all over the country. Too bad I didn't take the time to look inside it, wasn't it?"

She drew back from him, her eyes showing her pain. "Does it matter so much, Cal?" she asked hesitantly.

His expression was cold. He didn't even smile at her. "You lied to me."

"Not a lie," she protested. "Just . . . an omission."

"It amounts to the same thing," he said shortly.

"And the worst damned thing of all was that you did it for your sister. Was that what last night was about as well?" he added coldly.

She didn't even realize that her hand had moved until she felt the sting as it connected with his tanned cheek.

He caught her wrist in a bruising grasp, but he didn't hit her back.

"You'll have to let me know how much I owe you," he said in a stranger's mocking voice, a faint, harsh smile on the lips she'd kissed so ardently the night before. "I like to pay for my pleasures."

She couldn't have been more wounded if he'd slapped her. Her eyes misted with tears and she turned away.

"Where are you going?" he asked coldly. "The car's this way." He led the way to the car, put her inside and drove all the way back to the beach house without saying another word.

She went into the house like a zombie, thankful that no one seemed to be around, and headed straight for her bedroom. She'd no sooner walked inside and put down her purse than Jan came rushing in, her face hopeful, her eyes troubled.

"Did you talk to him?" she asked quickly, oblivious to the fact that the bedroom door was still open. "Did all that 'buttering up' work any miracles?" she added in a light tone, referring to the gentle teasing of days past, which had only been a joke between them.

However, to the coldly furious man standing at the doorway with Margie's suitcase in his hand, her words were the final confirmation of his suspicions.

"Come into the living room, both of you," Cannon said quietly. He turned and left the room abruptly.

Margie felt tears well up in her eyes and run down her cheeks while Jan stared at her uncomprehendingly.

"He knows who I am." She swallowed, and Jan's image blurred. "And what's worse, he thinks I was only playing up to him for your sake."

Jan's face crumpled. "You're in love with him," she whispered.

Margie managed to nod, before she broke down completely. "He's going to send us home, Jan." She wept on her sister's sympathetic shoulder. "I'm sorry, I'm so sorry!"

Suddenly Jan was the strong one, comforting, despite her own fears and apprehension. "It will be all right," she said, echoing the words Margie had so often spoken to her in times of distress. "It will all work out."

"I let you down."

Jan held her tighter. "Andy and I will find a way. It's you I'm worried about. Oh, Margie, forgive me for dragging you into this! If I'd stood up to him in the beginning . . . !"

But Margie wasn't listening. Her heart was breaking inside her shaking body.

Andy was glowering at Cannon when Margie and Jan joined them in the living room.

Cannon barely spared Margie a glance. He was smoking a cigarette, and never had Margie seen him look more unapproachable.

"I'm leaving for Chicago in the morning," he told them without preamble. "Under the circumstances, I think it would be wise if your . . . guests left for Atlanta at the same time," he advised Andy.

"My fiancée and her sister," Andy corrected, his eyes bright with anger.

"Over my dead body," Cannon returned coldly.

"If that's what it takes," Andy said agreeably.

"Andy, don't . . ." Jan said softly.

"I love you," the younger man told her, completely unembarrassed at the admission. "I won't have a life if it doesn't include you. If it means fighting my brother, all right. I'd rather lose his respect than your love."

Cannon shifted, glowering at Andy, but there was a glimmer of admiration in his dark eyes all the same.

"I'll go home with you," Andy said quietly, "and Jan will come with me. She still has vacation time coming. We'll hash it out there."

Cannon lifted the cigarette to his mouth. "Ganging up on me?" he muttered.

"I'll call in the neighbors, too, if I need to," Andy said with a weak smile. "I've got as much right to live with someone as you have to live alone. Just because you've gone sour on women, that doesn't mean I have to be doomed to bachelorhood."

"Women are treacherous," Cannon returned, and his eyes went straight to Margie.

"Why do you say that?"

"Don't you know who our houseguest is?" Cannon asked sarcastically, glancing toward his mother who was just joining the commotion.

"Of course I know who she is," Victorine said haughtily, glaring at her eldest. She put a comforting arm around Margie. "She's probably one of my favorite novelists."

Margie stiffened, and Victorine patted her comfortingly. "It's all right, dear," she said softly. "I've known from the beginning. I have all your books, you see." She glanced toward Cannon. "And if you'd ever once bothered opening one of them, you would have known her on sight. I did."

Cannon didn't smile. "What a pity someone didn't fill me in."

"And have given you another stick to beat Jan and Andy with?" Margie asked in a subdued tone. She smiled bitterly. "You might as well know it all, since this is confession time. No, Jan," she said when her sister started to speak, "Andy has the right to know it, too."

"Oh, I'm not arguing," Jan protested. She moved forward, just in front of Cannon. "It's my fault anyway. I begged Margie not to tell you what she did for a living. I had some crazy idea that I could let you think we were independently wealthy and . . ." She straightened, her eyes apologetic. "Mother died when I was born, and our grandmother McPherson took us in and raised us. She had to. Our father . . ." She paused and then plowed ahead. "Our father was an alcoholic. He drank us literally out of house and home, and when he was really high, he'd come and demand that Granny give us back to him. A couple of times," she recalled uneasily, "he tried to take us with him forcibly. Ashton being a small town, everyone knew about him. He was . . . notorious. We had a hard time at school because of that."

She tossed back her short hair and went ahead, and Margie had never been more proud of her. "When he died, and our grandmother followed him soon after, we had very little left. Barely enough to put Margie through two years of college. When she married Larry Silver, I had to live with them, and a lot . . . a lot of the problem with their marriage was me."

"That's not so, darling," Margie protested softly.

Jan laughed bitterly. "You know it is. I only make things worse for you." She looked back at Cannon. "Larry didn't carry insurance, and his parents wanted nothing to do with us at all—they were fairly well-to-do, but our family wasn't socially acceptable to them. So they turned their backs on us. Except to have their attorney demand their share of his small estate. He died intestate," she added. "So Margie was left with nothing—except me and a fistful of debts and horrible memories all around."

Jan took a deep breath. "Well, she took a job on the newspaper so that we wouldn't starve while I finished school. I won't tell you how many nights she was on the streets covering murders and drug busts and fires. The only job open, you see, was the police beat, so she took it."

Cannon's dark gaze went to Margie, and there was something in it that she couldn't endure. She dropped her eyes to the floor.

"She did that and wrote at night," Jan began again, "and one day she sent off a manuscript that an editor liked. The editor bought it, helped her polish it—and within months she made the best-seller list. I was so proud of her, I thought I'd die of it." She looked at her sister with love and pride in her expression. "I still am. And I wish I'd never asked Margie to hide the truth. We aren't rich. I make a fair salary at the law office where I work, and Margie is on her way to a Rolls Royce if there's any justice, but everything we've got she's sacrificed for. None of our people ever made the social register, and we aren't likely to, either." She lifted her small chin proudly. "But we're honest people for the most part, Mr. Van Dyne. I've done Andy a terrible injustice by not telling him the whole truth in the first place," she concluded. "And I've compounded that error by asking Margie to pretend to be something she's not. I'm very sorry about it all. And Margie and I will go home now. I hope we haven't caused you any great inconvenience." She looked at Andy with her heart in her eyes. "One thing was very true, though," she whispered. "I love you with all my heart."

Andy's face contorted. He went to her, crushing her to him, burying his face in her hair. "My God, what do I care who your people were?" he said in a husky voice. "I love you, you idiot!"

Margie's eyes filled with tears. At least Andy's love was sincere.

"I'll get my things together," Margie said quietly, turning away. "I'd very much appreciate it if some-one could drive me to the airport."

"Margie, you can come with us," Andy called curtly.

She shook her head. "I've got a deadline in two weeks," she said with gentle pride, "and the reason I went to New York was to sign the contract for a movie they're going to make of *Blazing Passion*."

"Oh, Margie, how wonderful!" Jan burst out.

"Sure," Margie laughed mirthlessly. "How wonderful." She turned back toward the stairs. "One more thing to make me stand out like a blot on the family escutcheon. . . ."

Cannon hadn't said a word, but his eyes were following her, and there was a kind of pain in his face that Victorine hadn't seen in years.

Her pale brown eyes looked worried as she tried to work out what to do. And all at once she smiled. It was so simple, really.

"Oh!" she cried, and let her body slump gracefully to the floor.

9

~~~~~~~~~~~~~~

Cannon carried his mother to her room, and grabbed the phone by the bed while Margie sat down and held the elderly woman's hand tightly.

"What are you doing?" Victorine asked in a ghostly whisper.

"Calling an ambulance," he said curtly.

"No!" Victorine argued, trying to sit up. "No, don't you . . . don't you dare!" she gasped for breath. "You're making it . . . worse!"

He murmured something forceful under his breath, gripping the receiver hard before slamming it back down again.

"Just get me . . . my pills," Victorine told him firmly, catching her breath. "In the drawer, here . . . and put one under . . . my tongue."

Cannon took out one of the tiny white tablets and dropped it obediently into his mother's mouth, just under her tongue. Then he stood beside Margie, with Jan and Andy stationed nervously at the foot of the bed, and waited impatiently to see if the medicine was going to help.

"I'd rather get you to a hospital," Cannon said curtly.

"And I'd rather . . . stay here," Victorine said breathlessly. She gripped Margie's fingers. "It's getting . . . better, now."

"Thank God," Cannon sighed. "Home for you," he added darkly. "I want you where I can get Howard when I need him."

"Howard . . . is our family doctor," Victorine told Margie. "And our good friend." She sighed, smiling her relief. "There, that's better."

"What can I bring you?" Margie asked softly.

"Not a thing, dear. But you're coming home with me. I need company, and Jan and Andrew are going to be much too busy to dawdle around the house with me."

Cannon's face clouded, darkened. But something flashed in his eyes that only his mother saw.

"I'm sorry, I can't," Margie replied quietly, knowing that it would hurt far too much to watch Cannon and not have the right to touch him, to love him.

"You may bring your typewriter with you," the elderly woman said firmly, "and the staff will look after you while you produce. In your spare time, you can do things with me. Can't she, Cannon?" she added with a hard glare.

He took a deep, short breath. "If it will keep you in the house, she's more than welcome."

"I can't . . . !" Margie cried, her eyes panic-stricken as they briefly met his and turned away again.

He rammed his hands in his pockets. "I won't be around that much, if that's what's stopping you," he said coldly.

"In that case, I'll come," Margie said, making her decision instantly. In a short space of time, Victorine had come to mean a great deal to her. If there were anything she could do for the older woman, she wouldn't hesitate.

"I'm glad that's all settled." Victorine sighed, leaning back on her pillows. "Now suppose you all go away and let me rest. Except Margie," she added, still gripping her slender hand. "I'll be fine, now."

Jan and Andy went reluctantly, but Cannon left the room immediately. Margie heard him leave the house shortly afterwards and he spent the rest of the day away.

He didn't come home for supper, either. Margie ate with Victorine off trays that Nina, the maid, provided. Andy and Jan ate in the kitchen, and then went to sit with Victorine while Margie packed her things and took a quick bath.

She'd just whipped her dark green robe around her body and was going down the hall from the bathroom to her own room when she froze.

Cannon was coming down the hall toward her, his face harder than ever, his eyes accusing.

She dropped her gaze and started past him, but

he moved, blocking her path. She looked up, scared of him all over again, and when he started to reach out a hand toward her, she jerked away from him.

His hand fell, and something dark and nameless appeared in his eyes as he looked at her, seeing all the old fears in her face, all the uncertainty that had been missing in the past few days.

"Sorry, honey," she drawled, back in character again. "I'm not available anymore. I've learned my lesson."

"Margie . . ." he began stiffly.

"No post mortems, okay?" she asked wearily. "Go back and make money, Mr. Tycoon, and leave me to my scandalous career. You don't have to worry, I won't stay in your home any longer than your mother needs me."

"For God's sake, will you listen to me?" he said sharply.

She shook her head, averting her eyes. "You don't have anything to say to me that I want to hear. You said it all this morning."

"Damn it, why didn't you tell me!"

Her eyes narrowed with pain. "Because I knew what would happen." She studied his broad, unyielding face with sad, hurting eyes. "And it did."

The words hung between them while he looked down at her, his expression giving nothing away. "You might have trusted me."

"I did trust a man, once," she reminded him quietly. "I forgot, for a little while, but I won't again. You'll never get close enough to hurt me again, Mr. Van Dyne. No man will." And she brushed past him before he realized what she was doing, and ran into her room.

The Van Dyne's Chicago home was a shock. Margie stared at it as if she'd never seen Victorian architecture before. Unlike her grandmother's wood home, this house was made of stone, and featured turrets and bay windows and ivy climbing gracefully up one side wall. Located far off the road and overlooking Lake Michigan, it was nestled among a grove of hardwood trees, a formidable rose garden and a maze of neatly trimmed hedges.

Jan had smiled brilliantly when Andy described the girls' Victorian home to Victorine, who burst out laughing.

"Now that is a coincidence," she'd told Margie with a smile. "Personally, I adore the architecture. It may have been a bit pretentious, but I prefer to think of it as a vanished art. Such style and attention to detail," she added with a sigh. "Lost forever."

Margie had agreed silently, but her mind was on other things—foremost among them the taciturn man at the wheel of the car. She hadn't paid attention to the Chicago skyline or the Sears tower or even the white sand beach that paralleled the highway. Her eyes had been helplessly drawn to the back of his dark head.

It had taken Margie and Jan several days to get settled in and familiar with the routine of the house. There was a daily maid named Anna who kept the house in working order, and her husband Jack doubled as gardener and chauffeur. There was a cook, Mrs. Summers, who was heavyset and jolly and served the best cakes Margie had ever eaten. Besides the staff, there was a swimming pool and patio out back near the rose garden, as well as a tennis court, not to mention enough wooded areas around the house to lure a wildlife enthusiast into their depths.

There was also a lake—like something out of a fairy tale, with swans and huge hardwood trees and a grassy area of flat land surrounding it. When Margie wasn't working on the book—which took most of her time as her deadline approached—or sitting with Victorine, that was where she could be found, with a tackle box and a bucket of worms and a fishing basket.

Jan and Andy were still doing their best to convince Cannon that their marriage wouldn't be the end of the world, but he wasn't showing any signs of altering his inflexible position. All that changed, however, the day Jan and Margie walked in on an interesting conversation Cannon was having with his mother in the living room.

He was standing at the window with his back to the door, formidable yet strangely lonely looking, in a dark blue, pin-striped vested suit that made him look every inch the corporate magnate.

Margie and Jan paused in the doorway, inadvertently eavesdropping.

"If you feel I'm too weak, I could get someone else to organize it, you know," Victorine was saying. Her eyes turned toward the girls then, suddenly gleaming. "As a matter of fact, I remember hearing that Jan did quite a bit of organizing for her boss. Didn't you, my dear?" she added, alerting Cannon to their presence.

Jan started. "Organizing?" she murmured. "Uh, well, I do organize quite a few dinner parties for him. His wife is an invalid, and he does a great deal of entertaining. . . ."

"You see?" Victorine said triumphantly. Jan and Margie stared at her.

Cannon moved away from the window, his hands jammed into his pockets, and stopped in front of Jan. "Can you organize a dinner party for twenty people, and do it in a week's time?" he asked bluntly, while his tone blatantly voiced his doubts.

"Why, yes," Jan said with disarming confidence. "If you'll give me a list of the people you want to invite." She grinned impishly. "I'll even make the seating arrangements so that business rivals don't go at it tooth and nail over the flan."

Involuntarily, he smiled, and the smile changed his whole look. "All right," he said.

Jan actually blushed, but she didn't lower her eyes. "I won't let you down, Cannon," she promised.

"He's going to let me do the party!" Jan exclaimed once she and Margie were out of earshot in the kitchen, and she hugged her sister enthusiastically. "Finally, he's giving me a chance to show him what I can do! Isn't it great?!"

"Great," Margie echoed with a smile. "Little does he know what he's just done," she added wickedly. "If I had a nickel for every party you'd organized . . ."

Jan giggled. "If this doesn't convince him that I know my way around society, nothing will." The smile faded. "Not that Andy and I are going to chuck our plans just because Cannon doesn't approve. Oh, Margie, you can't imagine how I felt at the beach house when Andy said he'd rather have me than Cannon's respect!"

"I think you're very lucky," Margie said softly, "to be loved that much."

Her tone was wistful, and it didn't escape Jan's notice. She moved closer, putting a sisterly arm around the taller woman. "Things will all come right for you, too. Didn't you see how Cannon was looking at you just now?"

Margie shrugged. "How he looks and how he feels are two different things. He didn't trust me. He didn't even give me the benefit of the doubt, or try to understand my point of view."

"Are you trying to understand his?" came the quiet reply. "He hasn't had a lot of reason to trust women, you know. Any more than you've had to trust men. It takes time."

Margie went to pour herself a cup of coffee, her face thoughtful. "Anyway," she said, "what do I have to offer? Notoriety—especially since that movie contract—a flamboyant image, a wild reputation that even my friends don't doubt . . . how would that fit in with the very conservative image his company projects? Can't you just see the board of directors having a field day?"

Jan eyed her sister, taking in the haggard look, the dark shadows under her eyes. It had been years since she'd seen Margie look like that, and it was disturbing.

"I don't think a man like Cannon Van Dyne would give a damn about what his board of directors said," Jan told her. "Not if he was in love."

Just the thought of it made Margie tingle, but she knew all too well the nature of Cannon's interest, and love didn't enter into what he felt for Margie. She laughed softly, her green eyes faintly amused.

"I can't imagine him in love," she murmured as she sipped her coffee. "It boggles the mind, doesn't it?"

"It doesn't boggle mine," Jan muttered. "But then, I'm not an old reporter like you. I'm not observant like you are; I'm not able to look at a man and tell he's crazy about a woman. Honest to goodness, Margie, everyone else can see it—why can't you?"

"See what?" Margie asked blandly.

Jan threw up her hands. "Never mind, never mind. I'm going to go upstairs and plot strategy. Let's see, I'll need a brace of dueling pistols, a few cannon . . ."

Margie laughed to herself, watching Jan go. It would be a blessing if Cannon changed his mind about Jan's potential.

She finished her coffee and put the cup in the sink just as the kitchen door opened and Cannon walked in, a smoking cigarette in hand. He paused in the doorway, effectively blocking the exit, and leaned back against the doorjamb.

"Want a cup of coffee?" she asked, and her face gave away nothing of the torment she was feeling.

He didn't answer immediately. His dark eyes were busy memorizing her, finding the small, tell-tale signs of her sleeplessness, of overwork. Her own eyes found the same signs on his hard features.

"Can Jan really organize dinner parties?" he asked point blank.

"Yes," she replied. She busied herself washing out her cup, and put it gently into the dish drainer. "She's done quite a lot of it in the past few years."

"Margie . . ." He moved closer, until she could feel his body heat behind her, as if he were touching every inch of her. His hands came down very gently on her shoulders and she jumped, as if they had burned her.

"Don't," he groaned, and his hands contracted. "Don't flinch when I touch you. I can't bear it."

She closed her eyes, involuntarily giving in, weakened by the delicious weight of his warm hands, the mingled scents of spicy cologne and tobacco.

"I wasn't flinching," she whispered. "You . . . startled me."

He was breathing roughly, the sound oddly loud in the kitchen. "You have to understand the way it's been with me all these years. My wife made a career of lying to me, right up until the night I found her with another man in our bedroom. . . . I'm not making excuses, but damn it, I'm not used to getting the truth from women. I thought you were Saint Joan," he concluded unevenly, "and you fell off the pedestal, that's all. From saint to nymph takes a bit of getting used to, especially for a cynic like me. I felt like a fool."

"Don't make the mistake of believing my publicity," she said, her voice level and cool. "I'm no more a nymphomaniac than you are a throwback to Victorian times. But it's the mold I fit into, and I can't break it, any more than you can break yours. Besides," she added with a short laugh, moving away from him, "our respective images are what make us successes. And they don't mix, Cannon. They'd never mix. It's just as well that things worked out the way they did."

"I don't like the way you sound," he remarked, watching her. "You're years too young to be cynical."

"I had a crash course," she replied. She folded her arms across her breasts. "My life hasn't been any bed of roses, but it's made me tough. And the first thing I learned was that if you let people get close, they can break you. I forgot that for a little while. But never again," she added, with a meaningful glance and a smile that never reached her cool green eyes.

"We had something very special," he replied, his voice quiet in the stillness, his gaze level and intense.

"Sex always seems special until the infatuation wears off," she returned.

"It wasn't sex," he corrected. "You may not know the difference, but I do. I wanted you in ways that had nothing to do with that very lovely body of yours."

She stared at him, her mind trying to make sense of the words and failing miserably. "It isn't wise to trust impulses," she murmured.

"You spent a great deal of time in my bed before we were interrupted that night," he replied. "Hardly an impulse on your part, was it?"

She felt her face flush, but she didn't look away. "I'd had quite a lot of wine," she hedged.

"Is that what you've convinced yourself happened?" he mused. "That I got you drunk and led you astray?" He paused to crush out his cigarette in an ashtray on the table. "I'm going to be out of town for a few days—a business trip I can't get out of. Maybe it's just as well. You might miss me."

She stared at him unobserved while he bent to the ashtray. She loved every hard line of his broad face, the way his thick hair curled just a little at his nape, the formidable size of his shoulders. He was so much a man, so big a part of her life, and she didn't want to think about days going by when she wouldn't at least have a glimpse of him at the dinner table or in the hallway at night. He'd been home every evening since they'd been in Chicago. She'd gotten . . . used to him being around. Her eyes dulled.

He turned, catching a glimpse of the sadness that lingered on her face. "Will you?" he asked, going close to catch her upper arms and tug her to him roughly.

"Will I what?" she murmured. Her eyes were on his wide, sensuous mouth and she barely heard him.

"Miss me."

Her lips parted involuntarily. Her fingers rested against his vest, but she didn't try to push him away.

"Suppose you kiss me goodbye?" he murmured. "Just for old time's sake."

"We haven't known each other long enough to qualify for that," she reminded him in a breathless tone.

"I've known you all my life, Margie," he said as his mouth opened and brushed her lips teasingly. "I've known you for a hundred years, and I've wanted you since day one . . . God, kiss me!"

He took her mouth, his arms riveting her body to the length of him, and she moaned softly as the magic washed over her. Her hands tangled in his thick hair, holding his mouth over hers as the kiss became more intimate, more demanding. Her body trembled with a fever and an ache that threatened to buckle her knees.

His tongue penetrated the sweet, dark recesses of her mouth in a rhythm that was blatantly suggestive while his hands traveled down from her breasts to her upper thighs and moved her hips slowly, sensuously against his.

She moaned again, arching sinuously with the motion of his hips, her nails biting into his shoulders. She wanted him, ached for him, and all the harsh words and accusations and recriminations were forgotten in the burst of passion he kindled in her slender body.

"I'm on fire for you," she whimpered involuntarily against his demanding mouth.

"How the hell do you think I feel?" he growled.

"I know you want me," she said in a voice that shook, and she looked up into his fierce eyes with blatant hunger in her own.

"Want you," he murmured. "What a tame word for a notorious romance author to use. Is that the best description you can come up with?"

She smiled slowly, sensuously, suddenly filled with confidence. "Are you going to talk, or kiss me?"

"You'd better hope I keep talking," he said, and made a very visible effort to control himself. "The kitchen table isn't the best place to make love, but it's looking more and more inviting to me right now."

She laughed softly. "What a wicked thought. I wonder if it's ever been used in a book?"

"Just hold it right there, lady," he said, and some of the old mischief was back in his dark eyes. "I draw the line at being used for research."

"I'd make it worth your while," she promised with blatant seduction in her voice, batting her eyelashes at him.

He laughed delightedly. "Would you? How exciting. Suppose you lie down on that kitchen table and we'll talk about it. . . ."

"Cannon!" Andy's voice came echoing down the hall, shattering the tenuous intimacy of the kitchen.

"Damn," Cannon muttered. "He's lying in wait for me."

"It's just as well," Margie observed. "God knows how I'd be able to work with splinters in my back."

He burst out laughing, and the sound was new

and sweet and delicious after the days of darkness and scowling. Margie felt girlishly happy, and her joy gave her a sudden vibrant beauty that made Cannon catch his breath.

"Why did you have to wait all this while to smile at me," he moaned, "and then choose a time when I'm an hour late for the airport?"

"I'll work on my timing while you're gone," she promised, and smiled at him again.

He touched her mouth with his finger. "Will you miss me?"

"Yes," she admitted, letting the barriers down.

"I'll miss you, too," he said. His eyes held hers. "When I get back, we'll talk."

She nodded. "I'd like that."

Then he was gone. And all the color seemed to go out of the world with him.

10

"Cannon should be home today," Victorine murmured on Friday, glancing up from her needlepoint.

Margie tried not to look excited. "I'm sure he's looking forward to the party tonight," she said mischievously. "Even if it's only to satisfy his curiosity about Jan's organizational talents."

"I think she's done a marvelous job," Victorine volunteered. "As good as I could have done myself."

Margie looked intently at the other woman. "Did you really have a heart attack?" she asked, voicing the question she'd been asking herself for the past week.

Victorine glanced up with innocent astonishment

firmly in place on her delicate features. "Me?" she asked.

Margie grinned. "Aren't you ashamed?"

"Not at all, dear." The older woman laughed. "Cannon was about to make one of the biggest mistakes of his life. I had to do something. And that was all I could come up with on the spur of the moment. How's the book coming, by the way?"

"I'm still a chapter short," Margie sighed. "I've been pounding and pounding, and that deadline is just a week away."

"It's probably my fault," Victorine said apologetically. "I'm sure being here has slowed you down considerably. But one thing I'm certain of—Jan will make a success of the party. And that will force Cannon's hand. He'll agree to the marriage, I promise you."

"I wish I had your confidence," Margie said with a faint smile. "Well, I'm off to the lake. I thought a little peace and quiet might perk up the old creative juices."

"They might perk up from another source," Victorine murmured, "if he weren't so bull-headed and inflexible and unable to admit he's human enough to make mistakes."

Margie only laughed. She got up, picked up her tackle box and walked down to the lake.

Cannon arrived only a half an hour before the dinner party was scheduled to begin, looking tired and older and drained of life.

Margie was just coming down the staircase in a

silver gown—the same gown she'd worn that magic night with him. He was on his way up the staircase, and when he happened to raise his head and see her, something explosive darkened his eyes, stiffened his posture.

"My God, you're beautiful," he said quietly. "Elegant, poised, glowing . . ."

She licked suddenly dry lips. "Thank you," she managed.

He moved further up the staircase, his dark eyes holding hers relentlessly until he was on the step below her.

He smelled of cologne and soap and tobacco, and she liked the dark, charcoal gray suit he was wearing; it emphasized the darkness of his hair, the olive complexion of his broad face.

"You . . . almost missed the party," she stammered. He made her nervous, this close.

"I missed my flight and had to catch another," he replied, but his eyes were on her body. "It's good to be back home," he murmured deeply. His fingers moved around to the back of her head, coaxing it toward his. "Is this lipstick smudgeproof?" he whispered as his mouth approached hers.

"I . . . I don't know," she whispered back.

His mouth parted, coaxing hers to open, to let him ease gently, slowly, into it, so that she could feel his warmth, breathe in his smoky fragrance. His breath was as ragged as hers, his heart beating wildly against the hands she'd pressed to his chest to steady herself.

"I missed you," he managed in a whisper, his hand tightening at her nape. "Oh, God, I missed you so . . . !"

It was the last straw. Her arms swept up and around his neck, and she heard his briefcase fall with a muffled thud. She could feel every hard line of his body against the softness of hers, feel the rough slam of his heart. He kissed her again, and the kiss went on and on until he was the only solid thing left in a world that had dropped out from under her shaky legs.

It was a long time before his ardent mouth lifted and she looked up with misty, half-open green eyes.

"Do you know how long it's been since I slept, since I could sleep? Do you know how it feels to lie in a bed alone and want someone with you until you feel as if you're being cut apart with a dull saw?"

"It won't work," she whispered, almost afraid to reach out for the happiness before her. Her eyes searched his, adoring him.

"I'm going to make it work, Margie," he said in a choked whisper, bending again to her mouth. "Darling . . ."

She parted her lips, lifting them up to his just as a door opened. He jerked back, his eyes blazing with mingled desire and frustration.

"Ready?" Jan asked, coming into view in a soft pink chiffon dress that flattered her complexion and the slender lines of her body. "Hi, Cannon! Welcome home," she added, watching him reluctantly move away from Margie to pick up the fallen briefcase. "The guests should be arriving any moment."

He sighed roughly, managing a weary smile for her. "If I'll do dressed as I am, honey, I'll put my briefcase upstairs and be right with you."

"You look very nice. Doesn't he, Margie?" Jan murmured with a dry glance at her flushed sister.

"Very nice," she echoed.

He held out a hand. "Help me put away the briefcase," he murmured, not bothering to hide the hunger in his face from Jan.

"Go ahead," Jan murmured, winking at Margie as she turned and went downstairs. "I'll handle everything down here," she added as the doorbell rang.

Another door opened and Andy came rushing out into the hall, his hand straightening his tie. He grinned at the tableau Cannon and Margie made, frozen in place on the staircase.

"Hi," he said. "You both look great. Jan downstairs? I'll find her. You two coming?" he called over his shoulder.

Cannon was still staring at Margie, who hadn't moved an inch. "In a few minutes. We've got to put away my briefcase first."

"You've got to what?" Andy burst out, stopping to gape at them.

"Oh, darling, our guests are here!" Jan called gaily, waving to him.

"Huh? Oh, of course!" Andy turned away, moving quickly down to join Jan in the hallway.

"We . . . we should go down," Margie whispered.

Cannon shook his dark head. "Not now. Not yet. I need you!"

She searched for something to say, and failed miserably.

Another door opened and closed and Victorine, in a long, peach-colored gown with a Victorian neckline, moved toward them with a raised eyebrow and a mischievous grin.

"Blocking traffic?" she murmured. "Why don't you two go and comb your hair?"

"Is that a better excuse than putting away my briefcase?" Cannon asked as she passed them.

"Your father and I used to use it all the time," she assured him. "You wouldn't mind if I congratulated Jan on her coming engagement . . . ?"

He sighed, watching the guests throng in the hall below. "Anything you want," he agreed, catching Margie's hand. "It looks as though she's done a superb job with the arrangements."

"Yes indeed," came the smug reply.

Cannon's hand tightened on Margie's as he tugged her back up the staircase and down the hall to his room, while her conscience warred with the desire in her body and she almost ran to keep up with him.

He opened the door and closed it behind them, dropping the briefcase even as he reached for her.

She gave in without a struggle, letting him put her on the soft, cream-colored coverlet. A moment later he came down beside her, his fingers tearing at the tie and the buttons of his shirt.

"You'll wrinkle it. . . ." she whispered shakily, helping him out of the jacket, the shirt.

"Damn the wrinkles," he said, his hands impatient as they stripped the silver gown to her waist. In the next moment he found her mouth hungrily with his own.

She could barely think when he finally lifted his head, her mouth slightly swollen from the fierce ardor of his lips, her body langorous, her legs trembling from the long, sweet contact with his.

"Stopping so soon?" she whispered unsteadily.

His eyes devoured her, taking in the disheveled glory of her long, dark hair which had come unpinned, the delicious bareness of her body above the waist.

"Well," he murmured with a faint grin, "we do have to put in an appearance downstairs."

She arched sinuously, smiling at the way his eyes darkened, following the movement.

"You little witch," he growled, moving his mouth down to cover the saucy little smile until he felt her lips quiver and part.

When he had released her mouth she cradled his head against her breasts and kissed his dark, cool hair. "I love you," she whispered.

He lifted his head, looking down at her with agony in his face. "I thought I'd killed your feeling for me," he admitted roughly. "I swear to God, I never meant to react that way. It was strictly an impulsive outburst, one I've regretted every minute since. I wanted to apologize—I tried to before we left Florida—but you wouldn't let me close enough." His eyes closed. "God, I thought you'd never let me get close to you again!"

She touched his mouth with soft fingers, her eyes adoring him. "I was afraid to," she admitted. "I was afraid my world and yours would never mix."

"We'll make them mix," he promised. His lips brushed against her bareness, making her tremble. "We're going to get married, Margie. I hope you'll meet me halfway on that issue, but if not, I don't really mind carrying you to the altar kicking and screaming. It would make great copy for all the morning editions—a really unique sendoff for your movie."

"That would really take the edge off your conservative image," she reminded him. "Your board of directors . . ."

He tilted her face up to his dark eyes. "I love you," he said in a curt, emphatic tone. "You, Mrs. Silver, you and your notorious alter ego. And nothing is as important as that in my life. Not the corporation, not my bank account, nothing!"

She felt the tears well up in her emerald eyes.

"Don't cry," he whispered, brushing the tears away with warm, loving lips. "Everything's going to work out beautifully."

"But it almost didn't," she pointed out.

"No," he admitted. "But fortunately, I have a mother with a devious mind and a big heart who knows me better than I know myself."

She gaped at him. "You knew about her faked heart attack?"

He grinned. "Of course I did. But you'll notice

that I went right along with it. I wanted you here
more than she did."

Her mouth pouted. "I don't see why. You spent
as much time as possible away from the
house. . . ."

"Hoping that you'd mind, that you'd miss me
half as much as I was missing you," he admitted in
a husky whisper. "It was almost enough that I could
see you, here in my house, or spy on you when you
went fishing."

"You watched me?"

"I had to," he confessed, pulling her against him,
and everything was revealed in his face. "Sometimes the hunger was so terrible, Margie."

"I know," she whispered. "All the color went out
of my world when you left it. . . ."

His mouth descended on hers slowly, achingly
tender, before she could get the rest of the words
out. He eased her against the pillows, his body
covering hers with a raging hunger.

Her fingers speared through his thick hair, holding him, cradling his head as the kiss deepened and
lengthened and his weight crushed her down into
the mattress.

"I need you," he said softly, his breath mingling
with hers. His fingers brushed down over her
breasts, her waist, her hips, savoring the smooth-
ness of skin, the firmness of muscle.

"They'll miss us," she managed. But the fever
was burning her, too, and all the hunger and all the
love was clamoring for expression, for fulfillment.

His hands came up to frame her face and his

eyes searched hers quietly, intently. "I can feel what you want," he said, his voice deep and slow in the stillness. "Just as you can feel how much I want you. I can't hide it. I can let you go—but it will feel like tearing off an arm, and I can't hide that, either. I've been a long time without a woman, and I want you so much I'm shaking with it."

She knew that. It made her feel strangely triumphant—that she could create the raging hunger, that she alone could satisfy it. She loved him beyond bearing, and despite her faint, lingering nervousness of allowing a man such intimate knowledge of her, she was past denying him.

She forced her taut muscles to relax, her hands to caress the hard contours of his body, her breath to slow and deepen.

"Please don't expect too much," she whispered, and a faint smile flowered on her mouth. "It's . . . going to be hard, even with you."

"I love you," he said simply. "Just concentrate on that, and remember that this is an expression of love."

A slow, sweet warmth spread over her body as he touched it, his eyes adoring, his face more tender than she'd ever seen it.

"Here," he murmured, rolling over on his back. "Touch me. Any way you want to. Be daring. Pretend you're one of your own heroines," he added wickedly.

She managed a smile as her fingers searched him. "My heroines are always passionately in love," she reminded him, "and they confine their amorous adventures to one man. I don't condone permissiveness."

"So I noticed," he murmured. "You know I finally read one of your books last week. It gave me hope. I decided that if you could write that ardently, you ought to be able to . . ."

"Hush," she whispered. She leaned down and kissed him, brushing her mouth over his with a lazy, loving pressure, smiling as she felt his chiseled lips move and open and coax hers into a deep, satisfying response.

"Who's doing this," she muttered, "you or me? I thought it was my turn."

His hands found her waist and lifted her over him, so that she was lying on his body. "Go ahead," he replied. "I'm only making a few . . . suggestions," he added with a gleam in his dark eyes as his hands caught her thighs and pressed her hips into his.

She moaned sharply, her eyes dilating at the sudden intimacy, and all the teasing stopped abruptly. He caught his fingers in her hair and brought her mouth down with deliberate sensuality, turning her, easing her onto her back, sliding down onto her throbbing body.

"Now," he whispered into her open mouth, "I'll show you what a woman is supposed to feel with her man. I'll make you tremble all over with hunger, and then I'll feed it. I'll give you such sweet pleasure that you'll hate the thought of another man's hands on your body. . . ."

"Cannon . . . !" she groaned as he moved, his hands touching her in new ways, in faintly shocking ways, his body kindling hers like dry wood, igniting sparks that burned her all over.

"Kiss me this way," he whispered roughly, his tongue fencing with hers in a sensuous rhythm as he eased the rest of the fabric from between them.

She felt the sudden contact with his bare flesh like a jolt of killing voltage, her eyes flying open, looking into his through a fog of pleasure.

"This is our beginning," he said. His hands lifted her, teasing her softness, and he smiled at the reaction he read in her face, in her misty green eyes. "This is how it's going to be for the rest of our lives. Let me show you . . . teach you. . . ."

She caught her breath, trying to tell him how much she loved him, how long she would love him, but a wave of pleasure hit her like whitecaps surging up on a beach, and all she could do was cling and cry and tremble like a vibrating string as he taught her how to please him. She whispered wildly, urgently, heard her own voice twisting into an echo of the pleasure her body was screaming, silvery and exquisitely sweet.

"This is love," he breathed into her mouth, and it was the last thing that penetrated her mind as her body seemed to catch in a hurricane of sensation, a frenzy of motion that tautened unbearably and then surged uncontrollably.

She cried out hoarsely, clinging, urging her body as close to his as physical limits would permit, and it was as if she lost herself completely in him. They became one, in a sense she'd read about but never really believed until now. And it was love. Total. Complete.

"I never knew," she whispered as she lay trembling in his arms.

He cradled her, pressing slow, tender kisses against her forehead, her closed eyelids, her cheeks, her swollen mouth. The wild pounding of their hearts began to calm slowly, and still he held her gently, like some priceless treasure.

"Neither did I, honey," he whispered at her mouth. He watched her eyes open and the look they exchanged was as intimate as the close contact of their sated bodies. "Because it was never with love. Until now."

She touched his face with wonder, tracing every line, and his eyes closed to savor her touch.

"I love you," she murmured, feeling the words as never before. "With my body. With my heart. With my soul. I want to give you children."

His eyes opened. His fingers smoothed back the hair at her temples, and they trembled. "I never dreamed that I could love like this," he confessed roughly. "You're as necessary to me as the air I breathe, do you know that?"

"It works both ways, my darling," she replied. She managed a shaky smile. "I want to give you everything."

"You just did," he reminded her, and a smile softened his face, his voice. "And now I suppose you'll expect me to do the honorable thing and marry you?"

"And spoil a beautiful friendship?" she asked, aghast.

He looked down his nose at her, cocking an

eyebrow. "I know you're a free spirit, Miss Famous Novelist," he told her. "But if you don't agree to marry me, right now, I'm going to carry you down those stairs and tell that dignified roomful of dinner guests that you're pregnant."

"Cannon Van Dyne!" she burst out, horrified. "You wouldn't!"

"Try me," he challenged. "My God, what a mass of contradictions you are. How many of your readers know what a Victorian mind you've got? It wouldn't bother me one damned bit to confess everything, but you blush at the thought!"

She laughed sheepishly. "And it's just the opposite with you," she remarked. "Oh, Cannon, your board of directors is going to be livid, do you realize that?"

"To hell with my board of directors. Are you going to marry me or not?" he murmured, kissing her roughly, slowly. "Think how shocked my mother would be if I told her that you could be pregnant. . . . And you could be," he breathed against her answering lips. "Already . . ." His hand flattened against her stomach.

"Impatient, aren't you?" she teased softly, but the thought made her tingle with excitement. She'd wanted children so much, for so long!

"I'll be forty next month," he murmured. "Would you really mind it happening so soon? If you would, I can . . ."

"No, I wouldn't mind," she said, silencing him with a kiss. "I want a family, too. And I have my grandmother's christening robe. . . ."

"There's a Van Dyne family christening bowl. . . ." he murmured back. His mouth smiled against hers. "I want ten."

"Ten . . . ? Oh!" she gasped as his hands moved.

"Bargain with me," he chuckled deeply. "How many do you want?"

The magic was working on her again. "Ten." she laughed. "Twelve. Fifteen. Anything you want—just kiss me!"

He laughed softly, triumphantly, as his mouth settled lovingly on hers.

The dinner guests had just eaten their way through the salad, and the first course was being served when Cannon and Margie walked into the dining room, hand in hand and grateful that they'd hardly been missed in the crowd.

Victorine got up and came forward to meet them. "It's about time," she scolded softly, just before she grinned. "Just look at yourselves. . . ."

"It was your suggestion," Cannon reminded her with a smug grin.

"Your hair looks worse than ever," his mother replied. "And I'll only forgive you if you say the magic word."

He lifted a bushy eyebrow. "Marriage?" he suggested dryly.

The elderly woman beamed and moved forward to hug Margie with real affection. "I told you I raised sensible sons." She laughed. "He knows a good thing when he sees it."

"Oh, it's not that," Margie confided with a

wicked glance at Cannon. "You see, I got him in trouble and now I have to marry him."

Victorine pursed her lips as she studied her son. "Have you no shame?" she asked him. "She'll think you're easy!"

He burst out laughing, hugging his mother to one side and Margie to the other. "Think? She knows it." He chuckled and winked at Margie. "Let's eat. I'm starving!"

Genuine Silhouette sterling silver bookmark for only $15.95!

What a beautiful way to hold your place in your current romance! This genuine sterling silver bookmark, with the distinctive Silhouette symbol in elegant black, measures 1½" long and 1" wide. It makes a beautiful gift for yourself, and for every romantic you know! And, at only $15.95 each, including all postage and handling charges, you'll want to order several now, while supplies last.

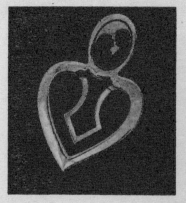

Send your name and address with check or money order for $15.95 per bookmark ordered to
Simon & Schuster Enterprises
120 Brighton Rd., P.O. Box 5020
Clifton, N.J. 07012
Attn: Bookmark

Bookmarks can be ordered pre-paid only. No charges will be accepted. Please allow 4-6 weeks for delivery.

N.Y. State Residents
Please Add Sales Tax

YOU'LL BE SWEPT AWAY
WITH SILHOUETTE DESIRE

$1.75 each

1 ☐ CORPORATE AFFAIR
James

2 ☐ LOVE'S SILVER WEB
Monet

3 ☐ WISE FOLLY
Clay

4 ☐ KISS AND TELL
Carey

5 ☐ WHEN LAST WE LOVED
Baker

6 ☐ A FRENCHMAN'S KISS
Mallory

7 ☐ NOT EVEN FOR LOVE
St. Claire

8 ☐ MAKE NO PROMISES
Dee

9 ☐ MOMENT IN TIME
Simms

10 ☐ WHENEVER I LOVE YOU
Smith

$1.95 each

11 ☐ VELVET TOUCH
James

12 ☐ THE COWBOY AND THE
LADY   Palmer

13 ☐ COME BACK, MY LOVE
Wallace

14 ☐ BLANKET OF STARS
Valley

15 ☐ SWEET BONDAGE
Vernon

16 ☐ DREAM COME TRUE
Major

17 ☐ OF PASSION BORN
Simms

18 ☐ SECOND HARVEST
Ross

19 ☐ LOVER IN PURSUIT
James

20 ☐ KING OF DIAMONDS
Allison

21 ☐ LOVE INTHE CHINA SEA
Baker

22 ☐ BITTERSWEET IN BERN
Durant

23 ☐ CONSTANT STRANGER
Sunshine

24 ☐ SHARED MOMENTS
Baxter

25 ☐ RENAISSANCE MAN
James

26 ☐ SEPTEMBER MORNING
Palmer

27 ☐ ON WINGS OF NIGHT
Conrad

28 ☐ PASSIONATE JOURNEY
Lovan

29 ☐ ENCHANTED DESERT
Michelle

30 ☐ PAST FORGETTING
Lind

31 ☐ RECKLESS PASSION
James

32 ☐ YESTERDAY'S DREAMS
Clay

38 ☐ SWEET SERENITY
Douglass

39 ☐ SHADOW OF BETRAYAL
Monet

40 ☐ GENTLE CONQUEST
Mallory

41 ☐ SEDUCTION BY DESIGN
St. Claire

42 ☐ ASK ME NO SECRETS
Stewart

43 ☐ A WILD, SWEET MAGIC
Simms

44 ☐ HEART OVER MIND West

45 ☐ EXPERIMENT IN LOVE Clay

46 ☐ HER GOLDEN EYES Chance

47 ☐ SILVER PROMISES Michelle

48 ☐ DREAM OF THE WEST
Powers

49 ☐ AFFAIR OF HONOR James

Silhouette Desire

50 ☐ FRIENDS AND LOVERS Palmer	68 ☐ SHADOW OF YESTERDAY Browning
51 ☐ SHADOW OF THE MOUNTAIN Lind	69 ☐ PASSION'S PORTRAIT Carey
52 ☐ EMBERS OF THE SUN Morgan	70 ☐ DINNER FOR TWO Victor
53 ☐ WINTER LADY Joyce	71 ☐ MAN OF THE HOUSE Joyce
54 ☐ IF EVER YOU NEED ME Fulford	72 ☐ NOBODY'S BABY Hart
55 ☐ TO TAME THE HUNTER James	73 ☐ A KISS REMEMBERED St. Claire
56 ☐ FLIP SIDE OF YESTERDAY Douglass	74 ☐ BEYOND FANTASY Douglass
57 ☐ NO PLACE FOR A WOMAN Michelle	75 ☐ CHASE THE CLOUDS McKenna
58 ☐ ONE NIGHT'S DECEPTION Mallory	76 ☐ STORMY SERENADE Michelle
59 ☐ TIME STANDS STILL Powers	77 ☐ SUMMER THUNDER Lowell
60 ☐ BETWEEN THE LINES Dennis	78 ☐ BLUEPRINT FOR RAPTURE Barber
61 ☐ ALL THE NIGHT LONG Simms	79 ☐ SO SWEET A MADNESS Simms
62 ☐ PASSIONATE SILENCE Monet	80 ☐ FIRE AND ICE Palmer
63 ☐ SHARE YOUR TOMORROWS Dee	81 ☐ OPENING BID Kennedy
64 ☐ SONATINA Milan	82 ☐ SUMMER SONG Clay
65 ☐ RECKLESS VENTURE Allison	83 ☐ HOME AT LAST Chance
66 ☐ THE FIERCE GENTLENESS Langtry	84 ☐ IN A MOMENT'S TIME Powers
67 ☐ GAMEMASTER James	

- -

SILHOUETTE DESIRE, Department SD/6
1230 Avenue of the Americas
New York, NY 10020

Please send me the books I have checked above. I am enclosing $_____
(please add 50¢ to cover postage and handling. NYS and NYC residents please add
appropriate sales tax.) Send check or money order—no cash or C.O.D's please.
Allow six weeks for delivery.

NAME _____

ADDRESS _____

CITY _____ STATE/ZIP _____

Get 6 new Silhouette Special Editions every month for a 15-day FREE trial!

Free Home Delivery, Free Previews, Free Bonus Books.
Silhouette Special Editions are a new kind of romance novel. These are big, powerful stories that will capture your imagination. They're longer, with fully developed characters and intricate plots that will hold you spellbound from the first page to the very last.

Each month we will send you six exciting *new* Silhouette Special Editions, just as soon as they are published. If you enjoy them as much as we think you will, pay the invoice enclosed with your shipment. **They're delivered right to your door with never a charge for postage or handling, and there's no obligation to buy anything at any time.** To start receiving Silhouette Special Editions regularly, mail the coupon below today.

Silhouette Special Edition

Love, passion and adventure will be yours FREE for 15 days... with Tapestry™ historical romances!

"Long before women could read and write, tapestries were used to record events and stories . . . especially the exploits of courageous knights and their ladies."

And now there's a new kind of tapestry...

In the pages of Tapestry™ romance novels, you'll find love, intrigue, and historical touches that really make the stories come alive!

You'll meet brave Guyon d'Arcy, a Norman knight . . . handsome Comte Andre de Crillon, a Huguenot royalist . . . rugged Branch Taggart, a feuding American rancher . . . and more. And on each journey back in time, you'll experience tender romance and searing passion . . . and learn about the way people lived and loved in earlier times than ours.

We think you'll be so delighted with Tapestry romances, you won't want to miss a single one! We'd like to send you 2 books each month, as soon as they are published, through our Tapestry Home Subscription Service.℠ Look them over for 15 days, free. If not delighted, simply return them and owe nothing. But if you enjoy them as much as we think you will, pay the invoice enclosed. There's never any additional charge for this convenient service — we pay all postage and handling costs.

To receive your Tapestry historical romances, fill out the coupon below and mail it to us today. You're on your way to all the love, passion, and adventure of times gone by!

HISTORICAL *Tapestry* ROMANCES

Tapestry™ is a trademark of Simon & Schuster.